D1342484

Please return / rene~
You can renew it at:
norlink.norfolk.gov.uk
or by telephone: 0344 800 8006
Please have your library card & PIN ready

NORFOLK LIBRARY
AND INFORMATION SERVICE

– g........ ....
school, then it looked like my sister had just been
voted this week's muppet.

Uh-oh…

Karen McCombie

BUTTERFLIES, BULLIES AND BAD, BAD HABITS

Welcome to the weird and wonderful world of Ally Love, age 13...

ALLY'S WORLD

■SCHOLASTIC

For Rebecca Petrie

(P.S. Hey Rebecca, hope you realize this means I'm expecting a dedication in return in one of your books!)

Scholastic Children's Books
An imprint of Scholastic Ltd
Euston House, 24 Eversholt Street
London, NW1 1DB, UK
Registered office: Westfield Road, Southam, Warwickshire, CV47 0RA
SCHOLASTIC and associated logos are trademarks and/or registered
trademarks of Scholastic Inc.

First published in the UK by Scholastic Ltd, 2001
This edition published in the UK by Scholastic Ltd, 2010

ISBN 978 1407 11760 7

Printed in the UK by CPI Bookmarque, Croydon, Surrey.
Papers used by Scholastic Children's Books are made from wood grown in
sustainable forests.

3 5 7 9 10 8 6 4 2

www.scholastic.co.uk/zone

Contents

PROLOGUE

Dear Mum,

How are you doing? We're all fine … now. It's been a funny old time for us all, but mostly, of course, for Rowan. Do you want the good news, or the bad news? Well, I guess I'd better choose, since you aren't able to answer. And since I can't send you this letter anyway.

I don't mean to make you feel guilty about that – I know you move about too much to have an address that we can write to. By the way, we got that letter from you today; the one from Frankfurt. Only Grandma got a bit funny when Linn showed it to her – she said that she didn't understand why you were going on about how "steely and grey" the sea was there, 'cause her boyfriend Stan's been over there lots of times for work and it's apparently nowhere near the sea. (Like I wrote before, Grandma's been seeing a lot of this Stan bloke, although she hasn't taken him round to meet us yet. And she'd kill me if she heard me describe him as her "boyfriend", although that's what he *is*.)

Anyway, Linn just shrugged and said it was probably just you being poetic, trying to make a boring, industrial town sound romantic for our sakes, but Grandma just tsk-tsk'd some more.

Oh, I'm forgetting about the good news/bad news stuff, aren't I? Well, the bad news is that Rowan got into a lot of trouble recently. I mean, a *lot*. Some of it was her fault and some of it was absolutely *not* her fault. Even the stuff that was her fault wasn't, if you see what I mean. Um ... well, you *will* see what I mean if you read all this stuff I've written down.

And the good news? I guess it's that we got it all sorted out. Not completely, but *kind* of sorted. In a funny sort of way.

I'm not telling this too well, am I? But if you love Rowan – and I know you do, wherever you are – you really need to read this.

Clear as a big bowl of porridge, I know.*

Love you lots,

Ally

(your Love Child No. 3)

* Blee! Porridge – Grandma's always on to us to eat that stuff. I'd rather eat *hamster* bedding.

Actually, do you think porridge is just juiced hamster bedding? I'd better not talk to Tor about this or he'll have a bunch of hay and stuff in the liquidizer before I can stop him...

Chapter 1

JUST DON'T MENTION THE PUPPIES...

"They're all DEAD!" yelled Tor, gushing tears like burst water pipe.

"Who's dead?" I asked, dumping my schoolbag down on the floor and running around the kitchen table to comfort my little brother.

I'd kind of dawdled on my way home from school. I'd stopped and chatted with my best friend Sandie at the corner of her street, and then she asked me to come up to her place and hang out for a bit. It seemed cool, it didn't seem like I'd miss much back home.

It seemed I was wrong.

"Who's all dead, Tor?" I repeated, crouching down and wrapping an arm around him.

On the other side of Tor, Rolf the dog was staring at him with big puzzled eyes, whining quietly in sympathy.

But Tor was inconsolable – beyond human speech. It was taking all his energy just to try to *breathe* between these great big, lung-busting sobs.

At that point Grandma bustled into the kitchen, with a box of man-size tissues (for Tor's non-man-size nose) and plonked them down on the table in front of him.

"There you go Tor, dear," she said in her usual kind-but-efficient way, ruffling his hair as she breezed past him. "Now, what about if I look out some carrots, and you can go and give the rabbits an extra treat?"

She's smart, our Grandma, she really is. She knows that the best way to humour Tor isn't to offer him sweets or crisps or staying up late – the quickest route to his heart is to spoil some of the (zillions of) fluffy, scaly or flippery inhabitants who happen to share our house. And it's pretty nice of her to do that, considering that she isn't actually too fond of animals (only don't tell Tor that).

Anyhow, I was relieved: if whatever was wrong could be solved by feeding carrotty titbits to the rabbits, then nothing that serious could have happened. I mean, I couldn't have lived with myself if a freak typhoon had hit the house and swallowed up my whole family while I was round at Sandie's watching telly and raiding her biscuit tin.

"Who's dead?" I whispered to Grandma, while I patted Tor on the back to try to get rid of the hiccups he'd got through too much crying.

As she started roughly chopping up carrots beside the sink, Grandma tilted her head, motioning me over to her.

"Penny the Labrador-cross – she lost all nine of her puppies," Grandma whispered.

"Ah, *Pet Rescue*," I nodded, getting the point.

It's one of Tor's favourite TV shows. But then, *every* TV show about animals is his favourite. He's got the times, channels and evenings when they're on all programmed into his head, and woe betide any of us if we want to watch anything on another channel while the *Ickle Cute Sick Wombat Show*, or whatever, is on. And if we've forgotten that one of those *was* on the viewing schedule, Tor has this funny little way of reminding us... Right before the theme tune starts, he disappears upstairs and runs back down with his Save the Seals T-shirt on (required uniform for the viewing of *every* animal show, and an item of clothing that's very hard to wash – there are a LOT of animal shows on every week, so the window of opportunity to smuggle the smelly thing out of his room and get it washed and dried is very small...).

"All the puppies got sick!" Tor hiccuped, as the sobs started to subside and he got enough breath back to talk.

"What made them sick?" I asked, going back to keep Tor company at the table.

"Just dog flu, I think," Grandma muttered matter-of-factly, obviously keen to get the subject closed as quickly as possible to prevent more Tor and Rolf howling duets.

"Parvo virus!" Tor corrected her, before blowing his nose loudly into a paper tissue that was big enough to engulf his whole face.

Behind him, I could see Grandma rolling her eyes. It must be weird to be put right by someone who's about sixty years younger than you.

"Ta-DAHHH!!"

I spun my head around towards the source of the cheerful whooping. It seemed pretty inappropriate when Penny – bless 'er – had just lost all nine puppies.

Rowan stood in the doorway of the kitchen, holding a T-shirt up to her chest, striking a model pose, with a great big grin slapped across her face. Though that went quick enough when she clocked the state our little brother was in.

"Uh-oh. Something died on *Pet Rescue*, didn't it?" she asked rhetorically, letting her arms, and the T-shirt, drop.

"Yes, but let's not talk about it any more, shall we?" said Grandma breezily. "Why don't you show us what you've got there, Rowan, dear? Is it a new top?"

The smile pinged back into place on Rowan's face.

"Yes – I went to Wood Green after school with Von and bought it. It's lovely, isn't it?"

Grandma pursed her lips slightly as she eyed up my sister's latest purchase. It wasn't that she disapproved of the top – a lilac T-shirt with an iridescent butterfly on the chest – it was more that she doesn't think too much of Von. I think she'd prefer it if Rowan hung out with a mate who was the same age (i.e. fifteen), and not the legally pub-friendly eighteen. And preferably a mate who didn't have a pierced nose and a tattoo (actually, Grandma doesn't know Von's got a tattoo – that would just be something *else* to disapprove of). All round, I think Grandma worries that Von will lead Rowan astray, but accompanying my sister shopping in Wood Green High Street doesn't seem all *that* wild and raucous to me.

"Gorgeous, isn't it?" Rowan beamed, rubbing her hand lovingly over the butterfly. "I've got a party a week on Saturday – I think I'll wear it to that."

Yeah, *right* – if she didn't buy herself about twelve other tops in the meantime. Rowan loves shopping – although, it has to be said, she isn't the type of girl that's going to help make many designers into millionaires in the near future. Her big kick is to get bargains, and she loves cruising the charity shops around Crouch End and picking up strange second-hand bits and pieces she can adapt and transform into something weird and hopefully wonderful (her trademark).

"And how much did that cost you?" asked Grandma, as she placed a plastic bowl of carrot chunks in front of a recovering Tor (he was down to only gentle snuffles now).

"Not much!" trilled Rowan, twirling around in her red velvet Chinese slippers.

(Our school uniform isn't too strict: a black blazer, a black or grey skirt or trousers, a white shirt, a stripy black, grey and white tie. But when it comes to shoes and coats and stuff, you can wear what you want and, believe me, my sister exploits that to its full potential. Last winter, she wore this ratty old fake leopard-skin coat that she'd got from the Cancer Research shop over her uniform. She thought it was very arty and cool. But it actually looked more like she'd been pounced on by a geriatric leopard which had then just *died* on her.)

"How much is not much?" I asked, wondering where she got the not-much-money from.

I knew for a fact that she was skint; she'd been

moaning that she'd blown all of her allowance by Wednesday, and Dad doesn't dish out our money till Saturday.

"Well, I had to borrow a tenner off Von," she shrugged. "So I'll have to butter up Dad and see if I can get an advance on next week's money."

"And then what are you going to do for cash *next* week?" I asked pointedly.

"Borrow off the *next* week's money?" she suggested blithely.

Rowan might be Queen Bargain-Hunter, but she still has zero common sense when it comes to actual pounds and pence. *Tor*'s got a better concept of money than her. Actually, *Rolf*'s probably got a better concept of money than her.

"What's wrong with *him*?" frowned Linn, taking us all by surprise as she strode into the kitchen.

We'd been so engrossed in Rowan's amazingly poor grasp of economics that no-one had heard our eldest sister come in.

"Guess!" I replied, glancing over at Tor with his red-rimmed eyes.

"Oh, *that*," said Linn, knowingly, and settled herself down on to the chair opposite mine. "You've got to stop watching that, Tor. There's always something dying on it, and it just upsets you. So, what died today?"

"Puppies," mumbled Tor, cuddling Rolf so tightly around the neck that he looked in danger of becoming another dead-dog statistic.

"Nine of them," I mouthed to Linn, holding the right number of fingers up in the air.

"Oh," she grimaced, acknowledging the higher than average mortality rate, and Tor's resulting grief.

"So, Grandma, is Dad around?" asked Rowan, blanking Linn and glancing up at the kitchen clock.

"Not yet," Grandma answered, while ushering Tor (and Rolf) out of the back door with the bowl of carrots. "He's working a bit later tonight – he's rushing to get a bike ready for someone's daughter's birthday tomorrow."

"Ooh, extra work!" Rowan smiled. "That means extra money – maybe Dad will just give me the ten pounds as a one-off, and not take it off my allowance!"

"Well, that wouldn't exactly be fair!" snapped Linn.

"Why isn't it fair?" Rowan asked her petulantly – sticking out her bottom lip ever so slightly.

(The way it works with Linn and Rowan is like this: Rowan comes up with a stupid, half thought-out, hare-brained scheme – and Linn shoots it down in flames. The End.)

"Think about it!" Linn sighed wearily. "If *you* get extra money off Dad, then he'd have to give me and Ally and Tor extra money too, wouldn't he?"

"Not necessarily..." mumbled Rowan, knowing she was beaten, but refusing to give in.

A big old slanging match was about to kick off in about two seconds flat, unless I came up with something to divert it.

"You're late home from school, Linn. Where've you been?" I asked, not bothering to fill her in with pointless little details like the fact that me and Rowan had only been in minutes before her ourselves.

"Me?" said Linn, arching her pale eyebrows and looking pretty pleased with herself. "*I* have been for an interview. And *I* have got myself a Saturday job!"

Linn had been going on about getting a Saturday job for ages. We all knew how much she really wanted a mobile phone, but as it didn't look like either Dad or Santa was going to get round to fixing her up with one of those in a hurry, she'd sussed that she was going to have to find a way to pay for it on her own. And now it looked like she had.

"Where did you get a job?" I asked, knowing instantly that it wasn't going to be stacking shelves in the supermarket. Linn wouldn't consider any job

12

where she might risk working up a sweat. She was too all-round prissy and neat for that.

"You know those clothes shops on Crouch Hill?" she asked.

"Oh, yes, they're all very nice!" Grandma marvelled, already impressed.

Please, I thought, *please let her say she's working as a cleaner in the pub opposite them!*

"I'm starting on Saturday at the one in the middle – Seasons," she said, smugly. "It's got more proper designer labels than the other shops..."

Oh, well, *not* the pub, then. Life isn't fair, sometimes, is it?

"Do they do staff discounts?" Grandma asked, her steely eyes lighting up, if I wasn't very much mistaken.

"Yes – I'll get fifteen per cent off. So that means I'll have lots of great new clothes, and plenty of money to spend on myself!" Linn boasted, smoothing down the front of her immaculately smooth white shirt with an air of self-satisfaction.

It's hard to be happy for someone when they're acting that pleased with themselves. It's not as if Linn doesn't have her moments of being likeable, it's just that she hides them pretty well. Instead, she just prefers to be smug and superior and gorgeous and perfect – a constant reminder to me and Rowan that we're ever so slightly inferior, lacking in gorgeousness and most definitely *im*perfect.

I glanced over at my fellow imperfect sister to see how she was taking Linn's news. Rowan's long, thick, dark hair was scraped back from her face with this mad metal hairband covered in little jewels: making her big brown eyes more obvious in her pale face. And right now those big brown eyes looked sad, and jealous and pathetic.

"So, Linn!" I said, turning to face Love Child *numero uno*. "You don't think Rowan should ask Dad for that money?"

"No," Linn frowned at me, wondering why we'd returned to the topic.

"Well, if *you're* going to be so rich now, why don't *you* lend Ro the money?!"

I already knew what the answer was going to be, but I couldn't resist being cheeky and asking it anyway.

"You must be joking! I'd nev—"

"Right!" said Grandma loudly, stepping in as referee. "Here, Rowan – this is from me ... but I want it back – a pound a week. OK?"

"Oh, thank you, Grandma!" gushed Rowan, running round the table to take the note Grandma was holding out and to give her a hug.

"I've had enough hassles today, what with dead

puppies," Grandma sighed, patting Rowan on the back, "and I don't want any more hassles over money. Do you three hear me?"

"Yes, Grandma," I nodded, hearing my words echoed by Rowan and Linn.

But as soon as her back was turned, Linn shot me a withering glance across the table. I nearly shot her one back, but I was trying too hard not to laugh at the sight of Rowan standing behind Linn's chair and pulling a face behind her back.

That's the trouble when me and my sisters start niggling at each other – we're a bit too big to get palmed off with carrots and bunny-feeding...

Chapter 2

FOR RICHER, FOR POORER...

When you're trying to watch a film, it's very hard to concentrate when there's a constant *thunk, thunk, thunketty-thunk* going on in the background.

"Dad, what are you doing? Why don't you come and watch this with us?" I asked, over the back of the sofa.

"No, it's OK, I've got these bills to go through," Dad muttered from the wonky writing desk in the corner of the room, not even looking up from the cheque book he was scribbling in.

I turned back to the screen, but the *thunketty-thunk* was really spoiling the mood. Out of the corner of my eye, I could see Linn's foot tapping in irritation. Half a second later, she'd slid Tor off her lap, grabbed a magazine off the floor, and walked round to Dad and the desk.

"There!" came her muffled voice, as she bent down out of sight and shoved a wodge of paper under the one short leg of the desk.

Brilliant – no more *thunketty-thunk* when Dad was writing.

"Thanks, Linn," smiled Dad. "Must get that fixed sometime…"

Ha. That's his catchphrase about everything in our rattling, crumbly, falling-down house.

"Come on, Dad, like Ally says, why don't you stop for a while?" Linn urged him, straightening up and standing beside him. "Come and watch the video with us!"

That's what the rest of us were doing – watching *A Bug's Life*, for Tor's sake. Before she'd escaped back to the sanity and calm of her own flat after tea, Grandma had come up with the smart idea of sticking on a film and letting Tor stay up a little later to watch it. As soon as she'd suggested it, I was rifling in the cupboard for something he'd love to see. Without a burst of cheerful Disney-ness before bedtime, Tor was bound to have bad dreams. And when he has bad dreams, it's usually *my* bed he crawls into in the middle of the night. And since there's usually a succession of cats and dogs making themselves comfortable on my duvet during the night, the further addition of a small boy generally means I have to sleep with half my body hanging out of my own bed.

"Yeah, come on, Dad!" said Rowan, switching the

video to pause. "You can even have this chair!"

Dad rubbed his stubbly chin at her offer, and then shook his head.

"No, it's OK. You three look too comfy to move," he replied, nodding over at Rowan and her lap full of snoring cats.

It was true; Eddie and Fluffy were dozing away happily, entangled in a blur of black and white fur so it was hard to see where one cat started and another cat ended.

"Anyhow – I've really got to get these bills out of the way tonight," Dad muttered more seriously, as he turned back to the paperwork. "Some of them are red ones..."

"Red's bad," said Tor, getting on his knees and staring at Dad over the back of the sofa, same as me.

"Yep," Dad nodded, "red is bad. Specially this one for the electricity. It's days old, but I only found it tonight..."

"How come?" I frowned.

"I saw the corner of it sticking out from under Winslet's blanket when I went to pat her earlier," Dad grinned.

Tor and I turned to the dog we were sharing sofa space with and frowned at her. Winslet snuffled guiltily, whipping her ears flat back and dropping her hairy head on to her hairy paws.

"What are you stealing bills for, Winslet? *Stupid* dog!" I told her off, waggling my finger in front of her nose.

She stared up at me with sorrowful eyes, knowing she'd done something wrong, even though all she heard was "Blah blah blah blah blah blah, Winslet? *Blah* blah!"

In a past life, Winslet must have been a pick-pocket. Usually she steals things that make vague sense: food (pretty straightforward), squeaky or fluffy pet toys (so Rolf and the cats can't have any fun) and random bits of clothing from us (preferably unwashed, but she isn't fussy – as long as it's chewable). But stealing letters was a new one. What was the point? Unless she was trying to teach herself to read...

"Are there *lots* of bills, Dad?" asked Linn, bending over the desk and trying to make sense of what was spread out on it.

"Yes, unfortunately. They've all kind of sprung on me at the same time, for some reason," said Dad, pushing the rolled-up sleeves of his checked shirt further up his arms. "And there's a whole load that's just landed on me for the shop too."

"But you'll manage to pay them all, won't you?" asked Rowan, with a slightly alarmed squeak to her voice.

"Urm, I'm sure I will," he said, unconvincingly. "Only I haven't quite figured out *how*, exactly…"

There was silence for a second, as we four Love children suddenly realized that while Dad might be smiling, he wasn't joking.

"Are we poor, Dad?" asked Tor, bluntly.

"Well, we're not rich," Dad laughed wryly. "And right now, we're *particularly* not rich. Put it that way!"

"Are we in trouble, Dad?" I asked, hoping he was going to tell me not to be so stupid.

Only he didn't.

"It's, um, more like – what do those banker-types say? – a cash-flow situation. Still, let's go crazy," he said, getting to his feet and clapping his hands together. "We've still got that big tub of ice cream in the freezer – why don't I get us all some and we'll cheer ourselves up?"

What a weird Thursday night this was turning out to be. First it was the drama with the puppies (RIP), then me and my sisters got all spiky with each other over Linn's supposedly good news, and now Dad was *not* quite managing to hide from us the fact that we were in a state of financial ruin.

"That's it," Linn murmured quietly, as soon as Dad had left the room. "I'm not going to take my allowance from Dad any more – I'll just manage on my wages from the shop…"

My head was a whirl (what's new?); what could I do to help?

"I'll get a Saturday job too!" I blurted out, determined that I'd start looking straight away.

"Mice!" said Tor.

"What?" I asked, my normal ability for interpreting Tor-speak failing me this once.

"I could ask my mice to have babies," he explained simply. "And I could sell them. But only to my *special* friends."

I could just see Tor now, rolling up to his friend's houses with his clipboard and pen, vetting their homes as suitable or not for his precious pets. He'd never be able to part with them – we'd just end up with gallons *more* mice scuttling about with the rest of the menagerie in his bedroom.

"Er, we'll talk about that later, Tor," said Linn hurriedly, obviously thinking along the same lines as me.

Then I realized that the only one of us that hadn't made a suggestion (useless or not) was Rowan.

"Ro?" I said, swivelling back round into a sitting position to look at her.

"We're … *poor*!" she gasped theatrically, clasping her hands to her chest.

There's one thing you can always count on with Rowan – if there's the slightest reason to flap, she'll flap. If there's a tizz to get in, she's your girl.

"Ro – it's OK," I tried to reassure her. "This isn't the Victorian times; we're not going to get sent to the poorhouse!"

I was trying to be funny (and failing). I saw the first hint of wateriness in Rowan's eyes and knew I'd have to act fast.

Lunging over, I grabbed the remote from the arm of her chair and pressed play.

"Just watch the movie and don't think about it," I ordered her.

Rowan blinked rapidly at the screen and did as she was told.

Honestly, sometimes she's so flaky you'd think Rowan was the youngest of us all, not the second oldest.

Only you know something? I was feeling pretty flaky and frightened too…

Chapter 3

ROWAN GOES WEIRD(ER)

"...and that's your assignment, boys and girls. Sorry to have kept you!"

Don't you hate it when teachers make you wait? (Especially last period on a Friday afternoon.) And don't you hate it if they call you "boys and girls" when you've been out of primary school for about a hundred years?

Just before I thudded my book shut and stuffed it in my bag, I glanced at the notes I'd just scribbled down and realized they were illegible. But I wasn't going to hang around and ask our English teacher, Mr Samuels, to go through it all again, not when the bell went five minutes ago and I knew Rowan would be waiting for me outside.

"*That* was boring," muttered Kyra, as we scrambled out of the door along with everyone else.

"Tell me about it!" I moaned, trying to do up the buckle of my bag as we walked.

"Do you fancy hanging out for a while?" Kyra

asked, wrinkling her little upturned nose at me questioningly. "Maybe go over to the park or something?"

"What's the matter – not seeing Richie?" I asked her, wondering if I was her second choice.

"Ricardo? No, I'm bored with him," she shrugged.

She'd been going out with Richie/Ricardo for about three weeks by then, and it was pretty funny to see how often she changed her mind about him. Either she was madly in love with him, or madly fed up with him and on the point of giving him the chuck.

It looked like he was on the downward spiral right then, and one of these days, I hoped it would stay that way – I thought he was a bit of an obnoxious creep, to be honest. It's like with the whole Richie/Ricardo name thing: just to impress her and sound more romantic or something, he told Kyra his name was Ricardo when she met him (even though I don't think anyone except maybe his granny's ever called him that). It wasn't till my mate Billy pointed it out, that I realized "Ricardo" was actually his buddy from school, otherwise known as Richie Esposito to his mates.

I mean, it would be like me telling some guy I fancied that he had to call me Alexandra, even though my full name is so unfamiliar to me that I wouldn't look round if someone yelled it out in the street.

"So what about it? The park?" Kyra repeated, as the front door of the school loomed closer.

"Nah," I shook my head, "I can't. Got to meet my sister and go and get some shopping up at the Broadway."

"Your sister? Which one?" asked Kyra, shoving some chewing gum in her mouth. "The pretty one or the weird one?"

Me and my weird sister arrived up at the Broadway, after walking up the road together in virtual silence.

It wasn't just the fact that we never do this kind of thing usually (me, Linn and Rowan *never* walk to or from school together – I guess because we see enough of each other at home, and because we tend to meet up with our own friends on the way. Well, me and Linn do anyway – Rowan doesn't actually have any proper mates at school). No, today, for some reason, Rowan was being *extra* weird, going all huffy and wobbly on me for keeping her waiting outside school, like I could *help* Mr Samuels being a pain and keeping my whole class back.

"Where've you been? I've been waiting on my

own for ages!" she'd narked at me.

Which was a lie on *two* counts: for one thing, it hadn't been ages, and for another thing, she wasn't on her own – there were still a couple of girls from her year kicking around the entrance when we got out. Anyway, what was she so scared of? Dying of boredom?

So I'd gone in a huff at her huffiness. (And yes, I know how dumb that sounds now.) But as we got closer to the shops, I had to resume communications.

"Where do we need to go? What's on the list?" I asked her.

"Um … it's all just vegetables," she replied, scanning Grandma's scrawly handwriting. "So, just the fruit and veg shop over there, I guess. Or do you think we should go round a few of them? Work out who's got the cheapest Brussels sprouts or something?"

I was just about to tell her she was being pathetic, when I sussed out that maybe *that* was what was up with her.

"But Ro, we don't have to *panic* about money – you heard what Dad said this morning at breakfast," I told her, as the green man beeped and we crossed over at the traffic lights towards the Clocktower.

I think Dad realized he'd freaked us all out the

night before. Even though we'd all pretended we were cool, and watched *A Bug's Life* and ate our ice cream and pretended everything was fine, he saw through it, I'm sure. That's why this morning, he'd taken the opportunity to tell us things weren't as black (or as red) as they might have seemed the night before.

"We just all need to be a bit careful when it comes to spending at the moment, that's all," he smiled round the table at us all. "So no buying any diamond tiaras this month, OK, girls?"

I was just about to cross at the next set of traffic lights when I realized I'd left Rowan behind.

So much for Dad's funny lecture and my reassurances – she was standing with her nose practically superglued to a gift-shop window dripping in trinkets.

"What are you looking at?" I asked her, half-expecting her to say "Everything...". It was Rowan's favourite shop in Crouch End, stacked floor to ceiling in jewellery, candelabras, painted glass doodahs and tasselly, silky lampshades.

"That CD rack," she muttered, pointing to a rectangular wicker and wire affair.

"What do you need a CD rack for? You've got one already," I pointed out, thinking of the plain white Perspex one she'd bought in a sale and customized by glueing on sunflowers cut out of a sheet of wrapping paper.

"Not for me," she sighed, leaving a fuzzy circle of steam on the window. "For Carla. For her birthday next week."

"Who's Carla?" I asked, trying to keep up with the mystifying twists and turns of Rowan's mind.

"Von's mate from college. The one whose party I'm going to next Saturday."

"Oh, *right*..." I mumbled, remembering her saying something about that when she was showing me and Grandma her new top the day before.

"I've been to her flat, down in Finsbury Park. It's really cool. And I thought that CD rack would be a good present to buy her. But I guess I'll have to go without taking her anything, since we're so skint at the moment..."

"She probably won't expect you to bring any- thing, since you're not like her best mate or anything," I pointed out, trying to console her.

It didn't seem to do the trick. Rowan still kept on staring through the window at the CD rack, like it was the Holy Grail.

"Or you could just *nick* it – *that* would be cheaper," I joked, in big, bad taste. "The only trouble is, if you stick something *that* shape up the front of your blazer, everyone's going to think you've got these huge, square boobs…"

OK, something was wrong. I knew it was a minus-one-out-of-ten kind of joke, but I did expect Rowan to giggle a bit, even if she followed it straight up by telling me how deeply rotten it was.

But Rowan stayed straight-faced, staring, staring, staring through that window…

Chapter 4

LINN GETS LUCKY (ONLY IT'S BAD LUCK)

We shouldn't have. We *really* shouldn't have. But we couldn't help ourselves...

"Look, there she is – wave!"

Tor did as he was told and waved frantically at Linn with his one free hand. The other was clutching a bag of pet-shop goodies (well, necessities – like us, the Love house menagerie were going to have to manage on short rations for a bit).

"Why is she looking at us funny?" he asked, squashing his nose flat up against the plate-glass window of Seasons clothes shop and breathing his steamy breath out like a halo on it.

"I think she's just shy, that's all. With it being her first day and everything," I murmured, grinning and sticking both thumbs up at our big sister.

Course she wasn't shy – just furious. Furious that we'd merrily ignored her order NOT to come and bother her on her first Saturday working at the shop. But she'd told us that at teatime the night before, and hey, it *could* just have slipped our minds. Well, it could have. Even though it hadn't.

("Shall we go home now?" I'd asked Tor, when we came out of the pet shop. "OK," he'd replied. "Or, shall we go round and see how Linn's getting on?" I'd ever-so-casually suggested. "OK," Tor had shrugged. See? It was that easy.)

There were no customers in Seasons at that precise moment – just rails and rails of expensive-looking clothes and two sales assistants. One was a middle-aged, very groomed woman, who was grumpily trying to force a roll of paper into the till. The other was Linn, who seemed like she was trying to look useful, straightening clothes that were already straight. At least, that was what her hands were doing. Her face was doing something completely different; twisted up into this weird, shocked frown thing. No wonder Tor thought she was looking funny.

"What's she saying?" he asked, breathing another steamy circle on to the glass.

With her neatly plucked blondish eyebrows practically bouncing up to meet her hairline, Linn was most definitely mouthing something silently at us.

"I don't know," I lied, waving all the harder at Linn, now I knew I was most definitely annoying her.

"I think she's saying something rude!" said Tor. "I think she's saying 'F—'"

"OK!" I interrupted him, before he translated Linn's words too loudly for a busy, bustling street.

I was just about to give up my most splendid game of embarrassing Linn and start hauling Tor homewards when I saw something I couldn't resist.

"Look, Tor – that other lady's gone into the back of the shop. Quick, let's run in and find out how Linn's getting on…"

Before he could say anything, I bundled my brother through the doorway of Seasons, into a world where Sting crooned through the sound system and the smell of pot pourri or fancy oils or something filled the air. It was all very laid-back and posh. In fact, the only thing spoiling the atmosphere was a small black cloud (invisible, of course, except to me) hovering in the middle of the shop, right above my tight-lipped sister.

"Go away! You'll get me sacked!" she growled, mean and low, while frantically casting her eyes back towards the counter, where I'd seen the middle-aged woman glide through a doorway seconds earlier.

"Don't be silly! How could you get sacked, just because your brother and sister have come in to say hello?"

It was a guess on my part that she couldn't get sacked just for that. But I figured that she *might* get sacked for working in such a snooty shop under false pretences. I mean, no matter how neat and trendy and together she appeared to be, having me and Tor turn up on her employer's doorstep looking like we were on our way to an eco-warrior, tree-saving, tunnel-digging road sabotage might just blow her style cred.

Poor Linn. She'd made a super-human effort to outdo herself that morning – it was as if she'd run the iron over everything from her super-smart Gap khakis right up to her hair (scraped and gelled back into a ponytail that was *so* tight it practically gave her a facelift). Then there was me, with my hair hanging shapeless and longish and in need of a wash-ish, wearing a grey T-shirt that had strange brown splodges on it from when I helped Tor creosote the rabbit hutches the weekend before, and a pair of combats and trainers that were both so battered they looked like they'd been in a war zone (well, when you're only aiming to trudge to the pet shop with your little brother on a Saturday morning, there doesn't seem much point getting glammed up).

However, my bag-lady look was still better than what Tor was wearing. I didn't realize his T-shirt

33

was on inside out and back-to-front till he took his sweatshirt off (hey, size labels worn under your chin *could* be the next big craze). His jeans might have looked all right from a distance, but the problem was that they were quite new, i.e. too big, and he'd forgotten to put a belt on, to hold them up. So the world at large was being treated to a lovely view of a sizeable chunk of Tor's Tigger pants.

"GO AWAY!" Linn hissed urgently.

OK. Now that her face was so close up to mine, I could see that she was really, truly mad at me. I was in serious danger of going just that weeny bit too far…

"Fine! No problem! We're going!" I said, all innocence, grabbing Tor by the hand and turning to head for the door. "*All* we wanted to do was wish you luck, but if *you* don't want—"

"Aaaarrrghhh!"

Can a scream ever be whispered? I'd never have thought so, but right then, Linn was definitely screaming quietly.

"What's wrong?" I asked, whipping round to see what was flipping her out.

"Uh-oh…" mumbled Tor, spotting what was wrong before I did.

Thanks to a hole somewhere in the plastic

bag Tor was carrying, there was a grainy trail of hamster food leading from the door to Linn's feet and back again, as we'd tried to make our exit.

"I'm sorry, Linn!" whined Tor, blinking hard at the mess on the pale grey carpet.

"Oh my God! How am I going to clean that up?" Linn stressed, her hands clutched over her nose and mouth.

"Hoover?" I suggested unhelpfully.

Linn narrowed her eyes at my flippant remark. I could practically feel the little arrows of hate that were shooting out of them.

Quickly, me and Tor scrambled for the door, casting another flurry of grain on to the carpet.

I did feel bad for her, honest I did. But as Tor and I trotted off down the Broadway towards home, I couldn't help smiling.

Rowan was going to *love* hearing about this...

Chapter 5

FOUR HOTDOGS AND A PACKET OF WINE GUMS PLEASE...

"Is this screen one or screen two?" I frowned at Chloe.

"Huh?" Chloe frowned back, walking into the room with a big bowl of popcorn in her arms, and staring at me, Sandie, Jen, Kellie and Salma, all sitting squashed in a row together.

"This *is* Finchley Warner Village, isn't it?" I continued, pointing at the huge blank screen in front of us.

"Yeah, when does the movie start?" asked Sandie, in a wobbly voice (she's no good at wind-ups, really she isn't).

"Uh, have we missed the ads?" said Jen, blinking hard at Chloe.

"Yeah, and what about the previews? Have we missed them?" said Kellie, all wide-eyed and innocent.

"Do we have time to get some hotdogs?" I continued, trying to keep a straight face.

"Wine Gums for me!" Salma grinned.

That started Jen off with the giggles (not a hard thing to do – Jen gets the giggles as often as the rest of us *breathe*). Not that she was laughing out loud, but I could feel her shoulders shaking right next to me. And it was infectious; there were snorts of suppressed sniggering coming from further along the big, wine-coloured leather sofa. Sandie and Kellie, I reckoned – Salma's really good at keeping it together during wind-ups.

Chloe narrowed her eyes at each of us in turn, her pale face scrunched in concentration as she tried to work out what we were on about. Then she looked at the big black monolith on the the other side of the room and finally twigged.

OK, so we were just goofing around and teasing her, but her new telly really was *vast*. I mean, *super*-vast.

"Ha, ha – I'm laughing so hard inside that it hurts," she muttered, with lots of eye-rolling at our pathetic gag about her back room turning into the latest multiplex.

For extra effect, she tossed her wavy red hair back and plonked the bowl of popcorn down on the table with a clatter. Chloe likes dramatic gestures.

Now that our feeble joke had been played out, Salma and Kellie wriggled off the sofa, grabbing a couple of overstuffed cushions each and settling themselves on the floor. And since we had more room, Jen, me and Sandie kind of expanded sideways, getting into suitable slobbing-out mode to watch whatever new DVD Chloe had grabbed from her dad's shop downstairs.

"Widescreen..." murmured Jen longingly, staring straight at her reflection on the black screen. "I wish *my* parents would buy one of these. Our TV is so small it gives me a migraine when I try to watch it for more than an hour at a time."

Tell us about it. Out of all of our houses, the least popular place to go to on one of our girls' film nights is round Jen's. Chloe's flat is the best because even though it doesn't look much from outside (it's right on the main road, right above her dad's shop and you have to get to it through a grungy back alley), it's really big and impressive once you're inside. *And* it has this separate TV room as well as a living room, so she doesn't have to plead with her mum and dad and brothers to get out when us lot are coming round.

My house is next favourite (even though our telly is so unreliable that sometimes it moves from being in colour to showing programmes in varying shades of *green*). All the girls love our comfy, sunshine-yellow living room with its squashy second-hand

38

sofa and armchairs and its clutter and cats and stuff (even though Chloe sometimes likes to moan about how the pet hairs make her allergic – but Chloe likes a good moan, full stop).

Sandie's place is OK, but her mum can be a bit much – she pops through about a million times whenever we're there and glued to a film. She offers us loads of cakes and nibbles and that kind of thing (which is great), but we all know (especially Sandie) that it's not just a case of her being thoughtful and nice; it's also because she wants to have a nosy and check that we're watching a nice safe fluffy movie and not some X-rated slasher flick (we save those for when we're round at one of the other houses). Poor Sandie – she gets absolutely mortified; you should see the shade of pink she turns when Mrs Walker hovers about in the doorway saying, "Any of you girls want another nummy hotty chocolate?" Urgh...

Salma's place is OK, but we can hardly ever go there, 'cause of all these manic tiny toddlers running about the place. Salma's mum got remarried a while back and has three-year-old twin girls. But Salma's nineteen-year-old sister has a little girl too, and she's always round at Salma's place as well. I mean, I like little kids and everything (well, I like Tor), but this lot are so LOUD. When you go round to see

Salma, you need earplugs 'cause of all these small, shouty hurricanes thundering about the house. And I can never tell them apart ("Rosa's the one who has the sulky screaming fits," Salma once tried to explain when I was at her place and getting all the toddlers' names muddled up. "Julia's the one who has hysterics if you try to pick her up, and Laurel is the one who just shouts all the time."). Rosa, Julia and Laurel – pretty names for miniature monsters. I still can't figure out which is which, but maybe that's 'cause they're always a blur of racing arms and legs. And I can't figure out how Salma manages to look so calm and serene all the time, considering she lives in a house that's about as relaxing as the middle of the M25 at rush hour.

A night at Kellie's is always a real laugh. She lives with her mum in a tiny flat, but the way her mum cooks, it's like she's feeding a really hungry rugby team. We turn up there on a GFN (Girls' Film Night), and guaranteed, get hit by an amazing smell of food as soon as we go in. Her mum makes mounds of all this Caribbean stuff and by the time we've watched a movie, our stomachs all look like we've swallowed a beach ball.

But back to Jen ... her parents are nice and friendly and everything – and they're quite cool 'cause they know a lot about music and bands and stuff – but they are the kind who disapprove of too much television; like it'll melt your brain or something. So they bought the world's titchiest telly just to make sure watching it is as little fun as possible. Torture, actually – it's true what Jen says about the migraine thing; I always come out of her house with a blinding headache after squeezing my eyes so hard to try and focus in on whatever was flickering over the screen. Her parents might think they're doing the right-on thing, but while they're stopping Jen and her sister from getting brain-melt from watching *Who Wants to be a Millionaire?* and *Emmerdale*, they should realize that they're permanently damaging their kids' vision into the bargain. Actually, maybe *that*'s why Jen has such tiny, button eyes ... maybe she was born with eyes as big as a bush baby's and then years of straining to look at a doll's-house-sized telly made them the way they are.

And if you ask me, Jen's mum and dad – bless 'em – must be really dense to think that Jen and her big sister Rachel don't just go and get their TV fix somewhere else. I mean, haven't they figured out that *that*'s why Jen spends so many evenings a week at Kellie's place in the next street? Maybe Mr and Mrs Hudson have this notion that Jen and Kellie are expanding their best-buddy teenage minds by studying origami or reading poetry to each other or something, but sorry – they're just curled up on the sofa in front of some soap with Kellie's lovely, cuddly mum and a family-sized pack of Hob-nobs.

But anyway ... back to Saturday night at Finchley Warner Village. I mean, Chloe's posh TV room.

"So what are we watching tonight, Chloe?" asked Sandie, her big blue eyes blinking questioningly at our friend. (Sandie's got a normal, watchable telly, so, see? My eye-strain=TV-size theory might *just* be right.)

"Well, I'm so angry with my dad," growled Chloe, as she crouched down in front of her flash new telly. "The new bunch of movies that were due in today? They're not going to be in till Monday now!"

I thought that was just a bit unfair. It's not like it was her dad's fault or anything, but then we were dealing with Chloe Brennan here, and I wasn't about to contradict her. She's a bit bolshy, is Chloe – one of those people who even when she's wrong, she's right, if you see what I mean. And after knowing her for a couple of years, I've come to realize that the easiest thing is just to shrug and let her believe whatever she wants to believe.

Of course, I don't always listen to my own

advice. It was like the week before, I had another go at trying to explain why me and Sandie hang out with Kyra now. Even as the words were coming out of my mouth, I knew I was wasting my time...

"Kyra was saying—" I'd started, forgetting for a second how much my other friends were still wary of her.

"Kyra Davies?" Chloe had spat out. "I still don't get why you bother with her. She's a total psycho."

Now, to be fair, that's what I thought of Kyra when she arrived at school recently. But also to be fair, I soon realized that all the loudmouth stuff she pulled in class was all part of her trying to cover up her awkwardness at being the New Girl. But try convincing *Chloe* of that, when she'd already made up her mind.

"Actually, it's like I've told you before: Kyra's OK when you get to know her," I'd shrugged, as Sandie stood back and let me do the talking. "*Isn't she, Sandie?*"

Sandie's nod was practically invisible to the naked eye. She obviously thought it was kind of pointless to push this with Chloe. Which I should have known too, if I had a brain.

"Kyra Davies is a psycho and she's got you two wrapped round her little finger," Chloe had announced, her arms crossed defiantly against her chest.

Behind her, Salma, Jen and Kellie just stood in silent agreement.

"But she—" I'd started to protest, feeling how unfair it was that none of my so-called mates were willing to give Kyra a second chance.

"She's a psycho," Chloe interrupted.

"She's not; she just—"

"She's a psycho."

"But Chloe—"

"She's a psycho."

I gave up then. The crazy thing is, Chloe and Kyra are kind of similar in a lot of ways (loud, bolshy, opinionated) which is why they don't particularly like each other. But it does bug me that Kellie and the others all just end up agreeing with Chloe for an easy life.

And it bugs me that I do it too. I mean, no matter how much I like her, there's no way I'd invite Kyra along to one of the GFNs (and that doesn't include the time she turned up at one uninvited, back when I still thought she was a psycho too). And that's all down to Chloe.

God, I'm pathetic, aren't I? For not standing up for what I believe in. Mind you, you haven't had Chloe stare at you with her dark eyes and her white cheeks all flushed and tetchy. It's like trying to argue with a she-lion. Or my sister Linn. In fact, I'd rather take my chances arguing with a lion with a grudge than argue with Chloe or Linn...

"So if there's no new movies, Chlo, what are we going to watch?" yawned Salma, stretching out across the floor and grabbing a handful of popcorn.

"I got the DVD of *The Sixth Sense* out," said Chloe, slipping the disc into one of the layers of matt black decks stacked under the new telly.

"I know we watched this ages ago when it came out on video, but the DVD has all this extra stuff, like showing you what all the clues were."

"Wow..." I heard myself muttering.

"Why 'wow'?" asked Jen, flopping her head around on the sofa to stare at me. "You guessed all the clues the first time around!"

"I didn't mean wow about the extras on the DVD," I grinned at her. "I mean wow about being able to afford all this stuff. How come your parents got this telly when the last one wasn't that old? My dad can't even afford to pay the bills this month!"

I don't mind mentioning money (or lack of it) in front of the girls. Although Chloe's family are pretty well off (obviously), and Jen and Sandie's parents seem OK that way, Salma and Kellie's families sometimes have it pretty tough. And although Chloe could act all show-offy about stuff in her own house, she never made the rest of us feel like our own houses were crummy by comparison. Well, not deliberately.

"Is everything OK?" asked Kellie, leaning up on her elbow and gazing at me with concern.

"Yeah, kind of," I shrugged.

(I could feel Sandie's eyes boring into me from the other end of the sofa; I hadn't sounded that casual when I'd been whingeing on about it on our way round here.)

"Isn't your dad's bike shop doing very well?" Chloe frowned.

"It's OK, I guess," I answered her, shrugging again. "I think we've all just got to be careful with money for a while. Like my sister Linn – she's got herself a Saturday job now. She just started today – in that clothes shop Seasons, just off the Broadway."

"Oooh, I'd love a job somewhere like that..." sighed Salma.

(Or anywhere else. As soon as Salma turns fourteen, she's planning on writing to every shop and business in a five-kilometre radius of Crouch End. It's not just the money she's after – it's just that it'll get her away from her flat full of sprogs for a whole, entire day.)

"Me too," I nodded. "In fact, I'd love a Saturday job right now!"

"Yeah? Well, I know where there's one going, if you're *that* desperate!" said Chloe, leaning back on her arms in front of the giganta-telly.

"Where?" I asked her, feeling my heart immediately race into a gallop.

"Just along the road, in that corny little card shop," Chloe replied, chucking her thumb to the right. "There was an ad in the window for a Saturday girl when I passed there this afternoon."

Instantly, I knew the one she meant. Crouch End is full of very trendy card and gift shops, but there are a couple of more old-fashioned card shops – the sort my Grandma likes to go into; the sort where she isn't going to tsk-tsk at the extortionate price of a card with a dried daisy glued to the front of it. ("Daylight robbery! You could make a meal for a family of five for the price of this!" she'd grumble, if me and Rowan ever dragged her into one of the fancier gift shops.)

"That would be brilliant!" I beamed, my mind already visualizing my dad's grateful expression when I announced I'd be helping supplement the family's income. Or at least, the fact that he wouldn't have to give me pocket money any more.

"Umm…"

I could hear Sandie's little squeak from the other end of the sofa and I knew she was about to say something that would burst my bubble. I'd know that negative-sounding "umm…" anywhere. That was the "umm…" that she did when I came back from the loos at the last end-of-term disco and told her excitedly that Ross Stewart had been eyeing me up and down (after her "umm…" she broke it to me that I had a metre of toilet paper attached to the heel of my shoe). And that was the "umm…" she did the time I told her I had a really good feeling about the magazine competition I'd just entered (after *that* "umm…" she pointed out the entry coupon with my address on it that was still lying on my bedside table, instead of being in the envelope I'd just posted off).

Basically, "umm…" meant "bummer".

"What's up?" Kellie asked Sandie, asking my question for me.

"Well, they wouldn't give Ally the job, would they?" Sandie muttered in a teeny-tiny voice. "I mean, she's not fourteen yet, is she?"

OK, so at the back of my mind I knew this. But it didn't make me any the less disappointed now that Sandie had pointed it out.

"Awww," muttered Jen, spotting how downbeat I suddenly looked (and felt) and putting her arm around me. "That's not fair, is it?"

"Well, there's an easy way around that!" Chloe announced.

"Huh? How?" I asked, hoping that Chloe would have an amazing plan.

"Lie!" Chloe grinned. "Go round there on Monday after school and just *say* you're fourteen!"

Somehow I'd hoped Chloe's amazing plan would be just a *little* bit more amazing than that.

The thing is, I know some people can lie really easily, but whenever *I* try to, bits of me start randomly twitching – which means people can work out pretty quickly that I'm fibbing for Britain, or else they assume I'm telling the truth but have a strange medical condition.

Either way, it's not good news.

Nope, lying just isn't for me.

"OK – I'll do it!" I heard myself saying. "Since it's for my dad..."

Hey, I thought. *Wouldn't Dad be proud if he could hear me? Not only am I planning on lying, but I also manage to keep my resolve for about two seconds flat, and then blame it all on him.*

What a lovely, trustworthy daughter.

Not.

Chapter 6

CHAMPIONSHIP FRETTING

Feeling terrible through lack of sleep is OK if you've done something amazing the night before.

Something amazing like going to a great party (not that I've been to many of those), or having all your girlfriends round for a sleepover and talking rubbish with them till dawn (done that plenty of times), or being abducted by friendly aliens who beam you out of your bed, take you on a speed-of-light tour of the entire galaxy and deposit you back in your bedroom in time for breakfast (it's never happened, but then you never know, do you?).

But sitting at the kitchen table this Sunday morning – with a plateful of cold and spongy scrambled eggs sitting uneaten in front of me – I felt truly terrible through lack of sleep, and it wasn't for an amazing reason at all. It was because I'd lain awake for hours, merrily fretting about money, lack of money, Saturday jobs and lying.

"Look, Ally, it's only a case of adding a few months to your age, and it *is* in a good cause!"

Chloe had said to me, before me and the other girls had left her house after our GFN (Girls' Film Night) the previous night. "Just don't make such a big deal of it!"

Don't make a big deal of it, don't make a big deal of it... I'd repeated silently in my head, as I lay poker-straight under the duvet.

But, of course, that's exactly what I did do, for hour after sleepless hour. Make a big deal about it, that is.

Outside my window, there were white lasers darting across the cloudy sky, thanks to some fancy event going on at Alexandra Palace. Normally, I'd have been perched on a chair, my nose practically pressed flat against the glass, staring at Ally Pally – all lit up like a fairytale castle on the hill – happily imagining what glitzy event was going on inside. But instead, I was running through a million problems in my head.

Like...

What if I went into the card shop on Monday after school, and the Card Shop Woman demanded proof of my age?

What if I went into the card shop on Monday after school, and the Card Shop Woman just some-how psychically *knew* that I was only thirteen?

What if I went into the card shop and couldn't

51

even *ask* about the job, because I was twitching so much due to the stress of lying about my age?

What if the Card Shop Woman gave me the job, but on my first day, some kind of Age-Checking Wardens from the council came in and demanded to know how old I really was?

Were there such things as Age-Checking Wardens? How could I find out if there were or not?

What if I was working there and people from my class came in and the Card Shop Woman worked out that they were only thirteen – so I must be too?

What if I went into the card shop on Monday after school and the job had already gone?

How could I help Dad out with money then?

How poor were we really?

How was Dad going to manage?

Where was Mum when we needed her…?

Oops, and I'd managed to work myself into a state about Mum, on top of everything else, which was really stupid.

That's the thing: me and my family pretty much try to think happy thoughts about Mum and where she is and what she's doing (Tor especially, but then he only knows the rose-tinted "Mum's-working-with-starving-sick-children-round-the-world" version of what happened anyway).

Somehow, during the last four years that she's been planet-hopping (just the one planet – earth – I mean; it's not like she's intergalactic or anything), Dad's been really good at getting us to think that way. "It's like this, girls," he once said to me, Rowan and Linn, "if she'd stayed here, she'd have been unhappy, even though she loves us all. If she's happier travelling the world, then we should be pleased for her – not sad. And she'll come back when she's ready…"

But there were times – like now – that I couldn't be happy that my hippy mum was off somewhere staring at stupid Roman ruins or tickling endangered sea turtles in Turkey or whatever she was doing. All that mattered at times like this was that she wasn't around. And no matter how many cheery letters and postcards she sent home, it didn't help.

And now, here I was, after a night of championship fretting, lost in this lack-of-sleep pool of misery. I was still staring down at the remains of my yukky eggs when I heard Dad suddenly rustle his Sunday paper and say something.

"What?"

That was it; that was all he said. For a second, I thought he must be talking to me. Quickly, I plastered a fake half-smile across my face – there was no way I wanted to add to Dad's troubles with my worries – when I realized he was talking to Tor.

"What?" Dad repeated, staring at my little brother across the big table. "What's up, Tor?"

Tor hadn't said anything, but then he didn't have to. He has this way of just staring at you till you realize almost telepathically that he's got something to tell you.

"Can Freddie come round and play this afternoon?" said Tor.

Focusing in on Tor, I noticed that he had a teeny tiny bit of bacon in one hand, pulled off the rasher on his plate. As he spoke, he dropped his hand under the table. When it arrived back up beside his unfinished breakfast, there was no bit of bacon.

"Freddie?" frowned Dad. "But I thought you weren't friends with him any more?"

"Am now," said Tor, his marble-like brown eyes gazing straight and steady at our dad.

Maybe Tor thought he could hypnotize Dad into not noticing the fact that he was feeding bits of breakfast to a small something under the table. Dad wasn't too hot on feeding any of the animals titbits like that. It wasn't as if he was worried about hygiene or anything like that; it was just that Dad was scared of Grandma. Grandma *really* disapproved of Rolf and Winslet and the cats hovering around and begging at teatime, and since she came round and made our tea and ate with us every weeknight, we had to try to make sure it didn't happen.

"Well, of course Freddie can come round and play," said Dad, saying nothing about the rapidly disappearing bacon (maybe Tor *had* managed to hypnotize him).

"But if you've asked him round to play in the garden, better do a check with the pooper-scooper first," said Linn, emerging from behind a Sunday fashion supplement at the far end of the table.

In my drowsy daze, I'd forgotten she was even there. But I wasn't so drowsy that I didn't notice Tor's hand disappearing under the table again. I half-fancied bending down to see who was wolfing down the brown-sauce-covered bacon, but I didn't want to draw Dad's attention to it and get Tor into any hassle.

"Oh God, yes, Linn – you're right. Last time Emily was round, she got poo on her shoe and I didn't hear the *end* of it from her mother…" said Dad, pulling a face.

"Rolf didn't mean it!" said Tor, passionately. "He never does it on the grass! He just had a funny tummy that day!"

Yeah, I thought, *probably had a funny tummy*

from eating too much bacon covered in brown sauce or whatever else Tor was smuggling to him that day...

But it wasn't Rolf getting the benefit of animal-unfriendly snacks this particular morning. While Tor was being (unusually) talkative and jumping to our dopey dog's defence, he was suddenly slacking from his duties as bacon-smuggler. As he pleaded Rolf's innocence, a small ginger paw appeared from under the table, scrabbling in the air for more treats.

It looked like Colin was doing an amazing balancing act (well, amazing for a cat with only three out of four legs). And it looked like Dad, who hated telling any of us off, was about to finally notice what Tor was up to.

Only it wasn't Tor that got the telling off. Surprise, surprise ... it was Rowan.

"Aaaaaarrr*uuuummpphhhh!*" she yawned, padding barefoot into the kitchen and yanking out the chair next to Tor. "Give us the toast, Ally!"

Rowan doesn't like getting up early at weekends. But when she does get up, at least she normally looks vaguely human. This morning, though, she looked like she'd been in the tumble dryer all night and come out all rumpled and puffy and creased. I decided I probably looked perky as a breakfast-show presenter next to her.

"Rowan, what time did you get in last night?" Dad suddenly asked her outright – none of the cheeky remarks like "Morning, Ro! Or should I say *evening*!" that he normally comes out with.

He said it in this weird, uptight tone of voice, too, and Dad *never* speaks like that to any of us. He's always really cool about what time we come in – he knows we'd never take the mickey and stay out later than we're supposed to (well, at least that was what I thought *then* – I was soon to see how wrong *that* was). And as for that weird tone in his voice; it kind of knocked me off balance a bit. Well, enough that my arm wobbled frozen in mid-air, still holding on to the plate of toast.

I noticed that two little spots of pink had appeared on Rowan's face. She obviously hadn't expected that stuff either.

"I wasn't late!" she mumbled, looking hurt.

"Ro – you were supposed to be home by eleven."

My arm was starting to hurt. I remembered it was still hovering, and tried to stick it down on the table as quietly as I could. I shot a look at Linn, who shot a look back. It seemed as if she was as stumped as me at what was going on.

"I ... I *was* back by eleven, Dad!" protested Rowan. "You ... you were asleep in front of the TV!"

Rowan's eyes were really dark underneath. I wondered if she was ill, then I realized that it was just eye make-up that had slithered south.

"Yep, I did fall asleep in front of the TV," said Dad, his skinny face taut and tense, "but I woke up when I heard you come in. And it was nearly half-past two, Ro..."

Me and Linn's eyes darted towards each other in shock. Rowan had broken the rules. Not just Dad's rules, I mean – *our* rules. Our rules that us girls never, *ever* give our sweet and funny and kind dad any grief, since he's had enough with Mum going off like she did.

Only our sweet and funny and kind dad didn't seem too sweet and funny and kind right now. He was doing textbook Stern Dad stuff: Chapter 11-and-a-quarter – "Getting Really Mad When Kids Stay Out Too Late".

"It's not fair!" Rowan yelped, screeching her chair out from under her and getting to her feet. "You're always telling me what to do! I can't take it any more!"

I felt like I was still dreaming. Where did Rowan get that from? When had Dad ever come across like a bossy parent? (Apart from right this minute, of course...)

"Ro!" exclaimed Dad, frowning at her with

concern. "Calm down! I was only worried about you! I mean, anything could have happened—"

"Get off my back!" wailed Rowan, her eyes getting all filmy and teary. "It's not fair – Von and Chazza can do whatever they want! No-one hassles *them*!"

"Rowan!" Dad protested. "Why are you talking like this? Like I said, I was just worried about—"

"Leave me alone!" Rowan choked out. "I'm just – I'm just sick of everyone interfering in my life! I wish everyone would just LEAVE ME ALONE!"

And with that, she flounced off. Well, as much as you can flounce in a pair of tartan flannelette pyjamas.

"You OK?" I asked Tor.

Tor nodded back, his face glum. He now had Colin on his lap and was cuddling him hard. Colin, meanwhile, was chewing on a whole rasher of bacon and looking blissfully happy.

"Well," muttered Dad, his face pinched and white, as if he'd been slapped in the face. "Better go and see what all *that* was about…"

As Dad got up slowly – sighing a bit, and not really looking at any of the rest of us – Linn burst into efficient action, just like Grandma would have done if she'd been here.

"Come on, Tor!" she smiled brightly. "Let's take

all this toast to Priory Park and feed the ducks!"

"But—" murmured Tor, staring at our big sister like she'd gone mad.

"No buts! Come on!" she smiled, grabbing an old plastic bag from the utility room, and chucking the plateful of toast straight into it. "Get your jacket, Tor!"

It was nice of Linn to try to bustle Tor out of the house and take his mind off what had just happened. The only thing was – as Tor and I both knew – there weren't any ducks at Priory Park. In fact, the only bit of water in the whole place was a little kids' paddling pool, and I didn't suppose the little kids' mums would take too kindly to Linn and Tor chucking hard bits of toast at their children.

The other reason Tor had said "but…" was obvious to me as soon as I saw Linn bundling Tor's arms into his anorak sleeves and ordering him to step into the red wellies she'd plonked in front of him.

But I didn't say anything – not when I saw Tor's grinning face.

It looked like he thought it was going to be fun to go out and feed invisible ducks still dressed in his Spiderman jim-jams.

*   *   *

Precious… Never in the history of dogdom has

there ever been a dog with a name that suits it less.

Sitting on the park bench, I couldn't even *hear* what Billy was wittering on about, his stupid dog was making such a racket.

"...so *Steven* goes to me, 'You're a total—"

Yap! Yappetty-yap! Yap!

"An' so *I* says to Steven, 'Well, you can just p—"

Yippetty-yap! Yap! Yap!

"An' then Hassan starts up and *he* says—"

Yap! Yap! Yippetty-yippetty yap! Yap! Yap! Yap! Yap!

I stared at Precious, willing the stupid poodle to shut up, but it didn't work. The yappy bundle of white fluff was meanwhile staring at Rolf and Winslet who were hunkered down on the grass, their scruffy heads resting between their front legs, looking like they wished with all their doggy hearts that it was physically possible to put their paws over their ears and drown out the noise.

"An' so *I* says, 'Hold on, Hassan, you don't know what's going on here!'"

Yippetty-yappetty yap! Yippetty-yippetty yap! Yap! Yap! Yap! Yap!

"Billy!" I yelp. "Never mind Hassan! *I* don't know what's going on – I can't hear you for Precious!"

Yippetty-yap! Yippetty-yippetty ... hmmphhh!

Reaching over, Billy had scooped up the hideous Precious with one hand and put his other hand over his mouth, clamping its over-worked jaws shut. Suddenly, it was as if peace and tranquillity had descended over the whole of the parkland around Alexandra Palace.

"Sorry," Billy grinned, holding Precious on his lap. "You know what he's like. He just gets excited when he sees your two…"

Poor Rolf and Winslet; I sometimes think that for them, playing with Precious must be as much fun as having a colony of fleas partying in your fur. Only louder.

But now that the world had gone quiet, "my two" were giving themselves a shake and a stretch (although not very far in the case of Winslet… Fate might have given her the long, hairy body of quite a substantial dog, but then it played a trick on her and gave her fun-size-Mars-bar legs).

"So anyway, what were you saying? About Steven and Hassan?"

"Well," said Billy, carrying on as if he didn't have an indignant poodle on his lap, growling quietly in protest at its mouth being clamped. "Like I was saying, there we were on Muswell Hill Broadway, arguing about all this stuff, when…"

I knew I was nodding at him, but really, my

mind was drifting away. I didn't want it to – in fact I really wanted to listen to Billy's tales of what him and his mates got up to the night before (and that didn't happen very often; not when all that they usually did was hang around somewhere talking about some Nintendo game and then go back to some guy's house and *play* some Nintendo game). Still, I wanted to give my brain a rest from everything that was running through it, and my mate Billy's boring Saturday night seemed like the perfect antidote.

But then off my head went again, getting in a tangle over the idea of asking about this job tomorrow (and lying); about Dad getting uptight with Ro (must be down to worrying about money, I'd decided, when I escaped the house with the dogs after Tor and Linn had left); about Rowan going crazy and shouty (who knew what was up with *her*?).

I gritted my teeth and tried again to forget all that stuff, and tune into whatever Billy was wittering on about.

"…and it was then that I saw Rowan," I suddenly heard Billy say.

"What about her?" I frowned at him.

"Well…" said Billy, looking sheepish.

It wasn't going to be good news, I could tell.

"…she looked pretty out of it, Ally."

"You mean *drunk*?" I asked, feeling my heart do a triple-jump lurch.

The thing is, I knew Rowan sneaked into pubs sometimes along with Von and Chazza (*I* knew it and *Linn* knew it – not Dad, of course), but I didn't think she necessarily *drank* when she was in one. Well, not *alcohol*, I mean.

"I *suppose* she was drunk," Billy shrugged uncertainly.

Oh God … it was getting worse.

"It was just that she was with this crowd, and those mates of hers – the ones that are all pierced –" Billy continued, not knowing what else to do since I'd gone quiet, "and she was staggering around a bit; like I say, kind of out of it."

He was swaying around on the bench, trying to do an impression of Rowan, I supposed. Any other time, I'd have started giggling, he looked so silly – especially when he was doing it while holding a bad-tempered dog on his lap that looked as if it was about to explode like a fur-covered time-bomb.

But this wasn't any other time, and I didn't laugh.

Rowan was maybe sometimes a little weird, but right now, something *super*-weird was going on with her…

Chapter 7

BIG WIGS AND PLASTIC HEARTS...

If you didn't know Kyra Davies, and you just saw a photo of her standing still – I mean, *totally* still, with no expression on her face and none of the posing, attitudey stuff she pulls – you'd probably think she was really cute and sweet.

Ha.

That's the trouble with first impressions. You see this girl that looks like Bambi (long skinny legs, fawn-coloured skin, little snub nose with sprinkles of freckles, almond eyes) and you decide she's *got* to be sweet and cute. Then she opens her big gob.

"Working in a card shop? Are you *joking*? That's sounds really naff!"

I was glad Sandie was sitting in-between us on the bench. I might have had to accidentally stamp on Kyra's foot. Hard.

I was beginning to wish I'd never told her about it. But it *was* Monday morning, and what are you meant to do during break but catch up on what's been going on over the weekend with your so-called mates?

"And you'd never get me to do a Saturday job, full stop," Kyra yawned, looking around the playground with a bored expression on her "cute" face. "It's bad enough being *here* all week; the last thing I'd want to do is spend part of my precious weekend in some *boring* shop serving *boring* people..."

Don't know where she got this "precious" weekend stuff from. She'd only just finished telling me and Sandie that she'd been bored to bits the last couple of days and that the high point had been phoning Ricardo to finish with him. (But then she got *so* bored by Sunday night, she ended up phoning him to say she'd changed her mind, even though she'd decided she doesn't like him very much. How desperate does that sound?)

"And if you're so skint, Ally, why don't you just ask your dad to give you more pocket money?" Kyra suggested blithely. "Your dad seems really nice – I'm sure he wouldn't say no..."

Doh! Spoken like someone who's never had to worry about money in their life.

"I'd love a Saturday job," Sandie sighed, before I had a chance to reply to Kyra's dopey comment. "But my parents would never let me..."

"How come?" asked Kyra.

"They just wouldn't," Sandie replied, dropping her head down and scuffing at the tarmac with the toe of her black shoe.

"Are they quite strict or something?" Kyra frowned, scrunching around in her seat to face Sandie, now that the conversation had taken a more interesting turn for her.

"They're not exactly *strict*..." Sandie shrugged, tucking her fine, straight hair behind her ears.

"They just treat Sandie like she's three, not thirteen," I explained.

Poor Sandie ... it's hard being the only child when you have parents like Mr and Mrs Walker who just want to staple you up in nice, safe bubble-wrap and smother you in love. I swear they'd never let her out of the house and into the big, bad, germ-filled world if it wasn't against the law. And they'd certainly never dream of letting their Perfect Little Princess spend her Saturdays stacking shelves in Tesco.

Kyra slumped slightly, looking disappointed. I think she'd hoped for something more dramatic than that.

"Oh, look," she said, suddenly perking up again. "There's your weird sister, Ally. What's she doing?"

I swivelled round and spotted Rowan straight away. In a bobbing sea of people dressed in black, grey and white school uniform, Rowan stood out like a luminous life-raft. Her blazer and long skirt might have been black, but her accessories certainly weren't. On her feet she was wearing her current favourites: her red velvet mules. With those, she had on clashing pink tights (ouch). Her schoolbag was something she'd made herself – a big, mental, fluffy orange number with a yellow felt buttercup-type thing hand-stitched on it. Shoved high on her nose was a pair of heart-shaped purple sunglasses that I hadn't seen before.

But it wasn't the explosion-in-a-Fruit-Pastille-factory colour scheme that made me stare at her (that was pretty standard Rowan stuff, after all) – it was what she was doing: just slapping the heel of her hand against her forehead over and over again.

"Is she all right?" asked Sandie, tilting her head to one side and peering at my sister.

"Back in a minute..." I muttered, getting up off the bench and making my way over to her.

Rowan saw me and stopped with the head-smacking before I got within talking range.

"Ro? You OK?" I asked, feeling a bit funny.

Funny, 'cause we hadn't spoken about what had happened with her and Dad at breakfast the day before. When I'd got back from walking the dogs, Dad had explained to us that Rowan hadn't been feeling well, and was sorry for upsetting everyone. He told us she felt very silly and that it would be a good idea if we pretended nothing had happened and acted like normal. Which was pretty hard for me, considering what Billy had just told me up at the park.

And I guess that's why I felt funny too; for the moment I was keeping that bit of information secret till I could figure out exactly what to do with it...

"Yeah, I'm fine," Rowan nodded, making all the tiny, coloured plastic butterfly clips in her hair glint in the sun.

"What was with the..."

I did the *thunk-thunk* thing with my palm against my forehead.

"Oh ... it was just ... nothing," Rowan replied hurriedly. "I ... um ... found out we've got a test next period and I haven't swotted for it."

She blinked at me through the purple lenses of her sunglasses.

Are they new? I found myself wondering.

Suddenly, I found myself a bit annoyed with Rowan. Not so much for being a drongo and forgetting about a test (well, I managed to forget a whole *project* not so long ago); it was just the fact that our family was supposed to be on a mission to save money just now, yet here was Rowan, with another new trinket for her collection of tat.

"When did you get those?" I asked, pointing my finger so close to her that she went cross-eyed.

"What – *these?*" she asked, fidgeting with one arm of her sunglasses and trying to sound all casual. "I've had them – oooh! – for ages!"

That wasn't true. And I knew that for two reasons: first, any time Rowan gets something new she parades it around me and Linn and Dad and everyone, like it's the most fantastic thing that's ever been invented; and second, those pink spots on her cheeks were getting pinker.

Yep, Rowan was definitely a liar, liar, though I didn't fancy checking to see if her pants were on fire.

"Um ... got to go! See if I can cram any revision for this test thingy..."

And with that, Rowan slipped inside the building, in a blur of technicolour.

"Well? How was the Weird One?" asked Kyra, as I moseyed on over to the bench again.

"OK – just freaked out about a test she's got," I shrugged.

I didn't really want to go into it any more with

Kyra, somehow. For her, whatever was going on with Rowan was just a bit of fun gossip, and I didn't want to do that to Rowan, even though I was kind of miffed with her right at that moment.

Just then, I felt Sandie link her arm around mine, and I knew that *she* knew there was more to it than what I'd just told Kyra. I looked at her questioning face and gave her arm a little squeeze (best-buddy sign-language for "I'll tell you later") and she mouthed me back a silent "OK".

Of course, Kyra didn't notice any of this – subtlety isn't really her thing. But then, just as I'd written her off as being too annoying to bother with this morning, she suddenly came out with something that made sense...

"Listen, Ally, I was thinking," she began, as she held out her hands and studied her nails. "If you're *really* up for this scuzzy Saturday job, why wait till after school to do something about it? It could be gone by then. Why don't you phone now? Before the end of break?"

Sometimes it takes someone else to state the obvious. So, in the space of five minutes, I'd borrowed a phone book from the school office, shoved some change in the public phone in the hall, and found myself connected to someone who sounded very batty indeed.

"Aloha!" crooned a woman's voice.

"Um … I'm not sure if I've got the right number," I mumbled, not expecting anyone Hawaiian to answer the phone.

"And who did you want, dear?"

"Um, I was trying to get through to Something Special…"

"Ooh, and you are through to Something Special, dear … something very special indeed!" tittered the voice.

I could instantly put a face to the voice now. Whenever I'd passed the Something Special card shop, I'd half-noticed the Grandma-aged woman who ran the place. She had the most amazing head of fancy blonde curls I'd ever seen. It looked like a (only slightly) scaled-down version of something Marie Antoinette might have worn. ("Wig…" Grandma had muttered sniffily, patting her own elegant grey crop one Saturday, when we'd been strolling past and I'd commented on the vision of blondeness.)

"Well," I gulped, and tried to continue, "I was wondering … the Saturday job. I was wondering…"

I wasn't doing this very well. Either my money was going to run out or the end-of-break bell was going to blast off above my head before I got any further. But I have this funny thing about phones sometimes. It's just that I find it really hard to communicate with someone I've never spoken to before, if I can't look them in the eyes. It's like I'm talking into this big void down the phone and I don't know what the other person is thinking at all, since I can't see their face to figure it out. Does that make sense?

I bit my lip and tried again, this time imagining Wig Woman and her towering pile of blonde curls at the other end of the line.

"I wondered if the Saturday gob was still jo-ing."

Nice! I winced, cringing at the mess I'd made of that. Even if the "gob" was still "jo-ing", she wasn't going to give it to someone who couldn't even speak.

"The Saturday job?" the Wig Woman trilled. "Yes, I still have a vacancy for that. Do you want to come in and see me about it?"

A wave of relief whooshed over me. Suddenly it seemed so easy. After stressing out the whole weekend since Chloe had first told me about it, here I was, being offered an interview. Just like that. Even after I got completely tongue-tied and nearly goofed up.

"Yeah … I mean, yes. Please. But I'm at school right now…"

"Fine! So why don't you just pop along this afternoon, when you finish?" Wig Woman suggested. "Just come in and ask for Mrs Merrill. And what's your name, dear?"

"Ally," I smiled stupidly, as if she could see me. "Ally Love."

"Ooh, how pretty!" cooed Wig Woman. "Look forward to seeing you later then, dear!"

And that was it. Perfect timing too, 'cause just as I put down the receiver (with my hand wobbling like it was made of rubber or something), the bell blasted off.

"I've got an interview!" I whispered to myself, setting off for my next class with a grin slapped right across my face. "I might get a job!"

As I started running up the stairs, with a million other people storming up behind me, something made me glance down through the stairwell. A certain sparkle that yanked my eyes like a magnet: Rowan was standing just outside the loo doors, holding something in her hands ... her new sunglasses, which looked – strangely – like they were now in two separate bits.

Serves her right, I thought, as the crush of people behind me shoved me further up the stairs. *If she blew money we can't afford on a stupid pair of sunglasses, she deserves it if they've been broken.*

But even if Rowan *did* deserve it, it still made me feel kind of gutted to see how totally sad she looked, holding a stupid, purple, plastic heart in each hand...

Chapter 8

ROWAN AND HER SPEED-OF-LIGHT MULES...

"I'll get the job…"

I yanked a leaf off the small branch I was holding in my hand.

"I'll get the job … *not*."

Yank – another leaf gone.

"I'll get the job…"

Yank.

"I'll get the job … *not*."

Yank.

It was five past four on Monday afternoon, and I was heading along the pavement towards Crouch End Broadway, mumbling to myself and leaving a trail of hedge bits in my wake. I'd been walking along, doing my usual tummy-flipping panic thing (about the interview and about the fact that I was about to lie to get the job), when I'd idly let my fingers trail along someone's garden hedge. I'd only meant to pull off one leaf, but tension must have made me stronger than usual and I ended up tugging out this whole sodding branch. I couldn't exactly stuff it back in, so I'd started with my alternative to the daisy petals and the "He loves me, he loves me not" routine, just to have something to concentrate on till I got to the card shop.

"I'll get the job…" I continued to mumble.

But before I could dissect the next chunk of shrubbery, I heard a horrible sound.

It's funny how you can recognize the sound of bullying, isn't it? It's the tone of the voices, even if you can't hear the exact words. It's like if a mate is shouting to you to wait for them, it sounds friendly, doesn't it? But when the yelling is about something nasty, it's like you can make out the poisonous atmosphere a kilometre away.

I glanced across the road, but it was hard to make out who was doing the bullying and who was on the receiving end; the traffic was madly busy and the whole of the opposite pavement – like the one I was walking along – was heaving with people in school uniforms, all streaming off towards home.

Suddenly, I forgot all about the bullying bellows, because right then, in the middle of everyone, I spotted a flash of bright pink, and could just make out Rowan, rushing past everyone; squeezing and excusing herself as she bolted ahead, her red velvet mules flippety-flapping at top speed.

Why's she hurrying so much? And where she

going? It's not the most obvious way to go home... I thought to myself, peering through the constant zoom of cars and buses and lorries and wondering if I could possibly get across the road at any time in the next month.

Glancing left, right, and left and right again, I saw a gap in the traffic and took it. But while I'd been concentrating on getting over the road, Rowan had conveniently vanished from view.

I stopped standing still like an idiot (being jostled and stood on wasn't the best fun in the world) and decided I should just get on with it – I had an interview to go to after all....

"...and over there are the condolences cards, although I do hate to sell those – it always means that a tragedy's happened to some poor family, doesn't it, dear?"

The Wig Woman – Mrs Merrill – rubbed her hands in contemplation and shook her head sadly. Normally, when someone shook their head that way, you'd expect to see some movement, but there was no mobile-hair action going on with Mrs Merrill's rock-hard locks. Those curls stayed stubbornly curled, without a bounce in sight. Yep, Grandma was right – it had to be a wig.

Mrs Merrill had done nothing but yatter at me

since the second I'd walked through the door and stammered my name, which was quite a relief, since all *I* had to do was nod and look interested.

The only dodgy moment had come when she'd pointed out a bowl full of birthstone keyrings for sale beside the cash register and asked me which one I was. I gulped and had to admit I didn't know. Mum probably told me what my birthstone was when I was little; when I wasn't paying attention because I (foolishly) supposed she'd always be around and that I could ask her things I'd forgotten whenever the fancy took me. Mrs Merrill seemed to frown a bit when I said I didn't know, and it did make me worry that that was one big black mark against me. Although her shop was full of pretty corny, sensible ranges of cards, she herself seemed to come from Planet Looney Tunes (the big, mad hair, the fact that she was singing "Oh I do Like to be Beside the SEASIDE!" at the top of her voice when I walked in), and I was sure knowledge of birthstone keyrings would figure high on her list of priorities.

"...and now the till. Have you ever worked one, dear?"

I dragged my eyes away Mrs Merrill's hairline (I was sure I could just see some normal grey hair poking out from under it) and tried to concentrate on what she was saying as she moved behind the counter. Behind her, the cars and buses hummed past outside the big plate-glass window.

"Um, no ... I haven't. Used a till, I mean," I shook my head.

Like a normal person, my long brown hair fell around my shoulders when I moved.

"Never mind! Won't take long for a sharp young mind to pick it up!" she said cheerfully.

Phew – it looked like being a novice in charge of a till full of money was less of a problem for Mrs Merrill than a shocking lack of knowledge about birthstone keyrings.

"All the buttons are very simple, and it's very easy to correct if you make a mistake. In fact, all you have to do..."

I stopped listening at that point. Not because I was bored, or I'm horribly rude or anything – it was just that I was curious to see Rowan on the other side of the road, with her mate Von. Von, dressed in black canvas army trousers and a long-sleeved black T-shirt, looked years older than Rowan in her (weird-around-the-edges) school uniform. I mean, I know Von is three years older than my fifteen-year-old sister, but somehow the age gap seemed even bigger – and maybe that was because Rowan looked like she was just a miserable little kid, the way she was mooching alongside Von, with her head hanging down.

"...so, what's your phone number, dear?" I heard, tuning back in to what Mrs Merrill was saying just at the right time.

Mustering a smile, I took the pen she was holding out to me and scribbled our number down on the pad where she'd already written my name.

Rowan would like this pen, I found myself thinking, as I doodled the green ink across the white paper, the huge baby-blue feathers glued to the top of it nearly tickling the end of my nose.

Finishing, I straightened up, handed the pen back to Mrs Merrill, and tried to sneak a peek out of the window again – but Rowan (and Von) were nowhere to be seen.

"Lovely! Well, I've a couple of other people to interview, Ally, dear," Mrs Merrill beamed, "but I'll give you a rinkle-tinkle as soon as I've made up my mind!"

It wasn't till I was halfway home – musing over what was going on with Rowan and wondering when exactly Mrs Merrill would give me a "rinkle-tinkle" – that I realized she'd never even bothered to ask me how old I was...

Chapter 9

HOME ALONE(ISH)

I really like all my friends, and they all really like me (hopefully). But there is one thing I prefer to do without them.

It's nothing drastic; nothing exciting. It's just that Chloe, Jen, Salma and Kellie always stay for school dinners (and maybe that's why the four of them are such a tight little clique), while I like to bumble on home and have lunch there. Sandie goes home too, but that's just 'cause her mum demands it – she can't bear not to see her "snookie-cookums" all the way from breakfast through to home-time, so doing anything but sharing a bowl of home-made soup with Mummy dearest is not an option. Kyra goes home too, but I don't think *her* mum calls her stuff like "snookie-cookums", not from the little she's told us about her mum and her drinking problems. Poor Kyra … every time she bugs me I should always remember that she's got *that* hassle going on in her life.

Anyhow, the reason I like to go home at

lunchtime is that, after the noise and hassle and crush of school, the house seems calm and cosy and lovely by comparison. And, much as I love Dad and everyone, it is kind of nice to go back to this quiet house, where there's only the sound of Radio One, me flicking through a magazine, and the odd purr and pant from the various cats and dogs.

Apart from the sound of the telly in the living room of course – that's where you'll find Rowan at lunchtimes; flicking channels with the remote control while eating her beetroot and cottage cheese sandwich, or whatever weird concoction she's slung together.

We (normally) get on great, me and Ro, and we can (normally) talk to each other for ages about stuff, but lunchtimes are funny. We both really like our own space, so while she does her TV thing, I leave her alone, and while I'm mooching in the kitchen with a magazine, she leaves *me* alone. Generally the only thing we say to each other at lunchtimes is "Hiya!" when we come in, and "See ya!" when whichever one of us heads back to school first. And that's just the way it seems to work.

But today was different. Today – Tuesday – I was twitching away at the table, *totally* not concentrating on the feature in front of me and staring through the kitchen door out into the lilac-coloured hall, wondering what was going on with my big (but not biggest) sister.

I couldn't put it off any longer. I couldn't put off ignoring what Billy had said, and ignoring how she'd flipped out at Dad on Sunday morning, and ignoring that I saw her looking all miserable with Von the day before…

So, I chucked the rest of my sandwich in the bin (i.e. Rolf, who was waiting patiently beside the bin with his mouth open and a hopeful expression on his doggy face), and walked through to the living room.

"All right?" I said, casually as I could, flopping down on to the sofa.

"*Yeah*," muttered Rowan, giving me a "Why are you through here?" glance from the armchair, where she and Winslet were sharing a peanut-butter-smeared Ryvita.

But I knew she wasn't all right. She had the news on, for goodness' sake. Rowan *never* has the news on. If there isn't some soap or chat-show type thing to watch, she'd rather stick on an old video of *Friends* or Tor's ancient *Bob the Builder* video than watch the news. It isn't that she doesn't give a hoot about the world and current affairs and stuff – it's just that it tends to upset her too much. You know how you see some stuff about a famine or a war and you see the kids and you feel sad? Well, Rowan doesn't just feel sad – she feels gutted, and then she uses up half the tissue reserves of the *world* sobbing over what's just happened.

So the fact that she was sitting glued to the news was *not* a good sign.

"What are you watching?" I asked stupidly, not sure how to start asking her what I wanted to ask her.

"The news," she replied, staring straight ahead at the screen, while Winslet took the last hunk of Ryvita out of her hand and swallowed it whole. Rowan didn't seem to notice. Or maybe she didn't care.

She didn't look herself today, I suddenly noticed. Her dark hair was scraped back into a ponytail with a dark scrunchie. Her tights were black. Her shoes, lying on the carpet beside the armchair where she'd kicked them off, were an old pair of black cotton Chinese pumps. In fact, the only glint about my normally ultra-glinty sister was one spangly yellow grip pinning her hair off her face in a side parting. And that was it.

"The news..." I repeated, even more stupidly.

I didn't know how to start with everything I had to say. So I didn't. I copped out.

"So ... are you ... OK just now?" I asked her

vaguely, hoping she'd make my life easy and just start pouring out whatever was bothering her.

Like, *yeah*.

"Course I'm OK. Don't I look OK?" she answered me, sounding a little snippy.

And before I could work up the courage to say anything else, she hit the volume button and started to look really interested in the news piece about the petro-chemical industry in Angola or wherever.

I knew I shouldn't have, but I gave up at that point. Maybe I should have tried harder, but until I'd worked out a smart way of getting her to talk, I thought I was probably just going to irritate her rather than help her.

"Well ... I'm heading back to school," I mumbled, pushing myself upright off the squashy sofa. "So ... see ya!"

"Yeah ... later!" she called, as I walked out into the hall.

"What's up with her?" I whispered to Rolf, who was now settling down for a doze on top of the wellies and shoes by the door after having his lunchtime snack – my leftover sandwich.

"Harrr-umfff," he replied, as I lifted my blazer off its hook and pulled it on.

Maybe it was just a doggy burp, but I felt like Rolf was agreeing with me.

"Exactly," I nodded down at him.

I reached up again to grab my bag, and stopped dead – frowning at a couple of white stringy blobs on the back of Ro's jacket. What were they?

I frowned some more and focused harder, then realized it was bits of chewing gum. I know I got some on my jeans a couple of times when morons had stuck gum on the seats on the bus, but how had Rowan managed to get some on her *back*?

Still, the mood Rowan was in, I wasn't about to ask her.

Chapter 10

GURGLES AND GROANS

Sandie was sitting bent over the desk in my room, her fair hair flopping forward and her tongue sticking out of the corner off her mouth as she concentrated.

The CD had finished, and even though Sandie was closer to my stereo than I was, she was too caught up in what she was doing to notice.

I was lying on my stomach on the bed, my head propped up in my hands, staring vaguely at Sandie and wondering if I could be bothered to get up and turn the tape over.

For a few seconds, the only sound in the room was my stomach gently gurgling. Grandma had made an excellent tea – home-made pizza and strawberry cheesecake (boy, was Sandie pleased she'd hung around this particular Wednesday night!) – but my stomach didn't seem too happy about it. It was making more noise than the groany old water pipes that rattled the length of our house whenever you even *looked* at a tap, never mind turn one on.

"Greeee-oooow-*nooooof*!!"

That was it. That was enough with the stupid stomach noises.

"Sandie – go and stick on a different CD!" I begged her, since I had zilch energy to move from my comfy position.

"In a minute..." mumbled Sandie.

"But Sandie, it's too quiet in here. We need music!"

"There!" Sandie announced, suddenly sitting up straight and grinning at me. "What do you think?"

She was holding out her hands towards me, wiggling her fingers wide, to show off the new nail varnish she'd just put on (a freebie that she peeled off the front of the magazine she'd brought round with her).

"Yuk!" I said, automatically scrunching up my nose. "It looks like your fingers have got the plague!"

I didn't mean to be horrible – it's just that I couldn't figure out how anyone could sit in a lab or wherever they made nail varnish, and decide that the most groovy colour they could come up with was a kind of sickly grey-blue (not forgetting the special sheeny-shiny effect it had, like the sheeny-shiny lustre of an oil spill...).

"Yeah, it *is* pretty yukky," Sandie agreed with

me, replacing her smile with a little scowl. "Got any nail-varnish remover?"

"Linn'll have some – I'll get it off her before you go home," I mumbled, sinking my head down into my hands so that my knuckles squished my cheeks further up my face.

"You look like a cross between a frog and a chipmunk when you do that," said Sandie.

"Thank you," I mumbled, without rearranging my face in any way.

"Do you want me to try out one of the quizzes on you?" asked Sandie, pointing to the magazine in front of her.

"Go on, then," I muttered, without much enthusiasm.

Reaching over to the CD player, Sandie expertly switched CDs, while flicking her hand through the pages of the magazine with the other.

"Here's one!" she announced, letting her finger drop on one page, while the music started up behind her. "OK... so this one's called '*Are You A Happy Bunny?*'"

"Shouldn't you be trying this out on Cilla instead of me?" I said grumpily, thinking of the fat, fluffy, carrot-cruncher who'd be snoozing out in her rabbit hutch as we spoke.

"Ha, ha," said Sandie brightly. "Right, so the

first question is… *'There's something making you feel a bit blue just now. Is it … a) Worrying about your sister, b) Stressing out about the fact that the woman in the card shop hasn't phoned you back yet, or c) Both of these'*."

Now it was my turn for the fake laugh.

"Ha, ha," I said, dropping my elbows and flopping my head down on the bed, so that my face was buried in my cloud-patterned duvet.

"But it's true, isn't it? You're getting all stressed out about the job thing, *and* about Rowan, aren't you?" I heard Sandie ask.

"Yuff," I mumbled, my words (well, *word*) getting muffled in amongst the cotton clouds.

She was right. I was letting it all get me down, and apart from telling Sandie about it, I was being truly rubbish and doing nothing to sort any of it out. And, bless her, though Sandie's a great listener and brilliant at being sympathetic, she's not that great at giving me any advice.

"I mean, with the lady at the card shop – why don't you just go in after school tomorrow, and ask her if you've got the job or not?" Sandie suggested.

Because I couldn't bear the humiliation of her telling me to my face that I haven't got it, I thought to myself. *I'd be so embarrassed that I'd have to cross the road every time I'm passing by the shop...*

Sandie was silent for a bit, giving me the chance to say something back, but I didn't. I just made a non-committal noise.

"Humf," I grunted.

"And, with Rowan, why don't you just tell your dad about Billy seeing her drunk on Saturday, and that you're worried about how weird she's being?"

Because Billy is lovely but he can be a real doughball sometimes, and what if he got it wrong? And what if I've put two and two together and come up with something completely stupid? I mean, if she was getting into booze or something, would those really be the symptoms? Flying off the handle on Sunday morning maybe, but dressing nearly normally (like today) and looking all annoyed when I saw her with Von (like yesterday) doesn't mean there's anything serious going on with her...

Look at that – my mind is very good at worrying (I think I'd get an A+ if they did exams in Worrying). It's just that my mouth is sometimes not very good at saying it all.

"Humf," I repeated.

Then the phone jangled into life, which in turn jangled me out of my soggy mood.

"Why is no-one answering that?" I asked, lifting

my head up.

Dad was at his evening class (well, it's actually his line-dancing class, but that's almost too embarrassing to mention), but last time I looked, Rowan and Linn were both downstairs in the living room with Tor.

The phone kept trilling away.

"My stupid sisters!" I grumbled, pushing myself off the bed and stomping my way to the door and down the attic steps.

But just as I reached the first-floor landing, the ringing stopped, and so did I.

"Hello, this is Tor. Who are you?" I heard my little brother say.

I hovered about in case it was Billy. Sometimes, me and Billy only see each other once a week, when we meet up with the dogs on Sunday morning. But we speak to each other loads – usually 'cause Billy gets bored easily and likes to phone me up and tell me how bored he is.

"You sound funny," I heard Tor giggle.

What was Billy doing? *Yodelling* down the phone?

"I'm seven. How old are you?"

Well, it wasn't Billy. Tor knew that he was thirteen, same age as me.

"Huh? She's in her bedroom."

I glanced around the upstairs hall and saw no light shining under Rowan's door, and Linn's door had been wide open into a darkened room when I sped down here, so I quickly worked out (duh!) that the call *had* to be for me. I started down the last flight of stairs, looking over the bannister at Tor's dark head bobbing below.

"Uh-huh. OK. I'll shout for her. *Alllllllyyyy!*"

"I'm coming! I'm coming!" I said out loud, and mouthed "Who is it?" at him.

Tor shrugged and held out the phone towards me, but just as I got within two footsteps of him, I saw his eyes light up and he thudded the receiver back to his ear again.

"Are you the old lady with the w—"

In one smooth move I yanked the phone away from him and closed my other hand over his mouth.

"Hello?" I said tentatively.

"Is that Miss Love?" came a sing-song voice that could only belong to Mrs Merrill.

"Yes," I answered breathlessly, hoping against hope that she a) was going to tell me good news, and b) hadn't worked out what my darling little brother had been about to say.

"That was the Wig Woman, wasn't it?" Tor asked me, when I finally hung up the phone and let go of his mouth.

"Don't call her that!" I reprimanded him.

"Why not?" he blinked at me. "You did at teatime."

Oops.

He was right. I'd been moaning to Sandie – when only her, me and Tor were left at the table having our second helpings of what was left of the cheese-cake – and I'd called Mrs Merrill Wig Woman.

"Well, we can't call her that any more," I smiled at him. "It's rude, and anyway, her name is Mrs Merrill."

After all, I couldn't be horrible about her now. Not when the lovely, gorgeous, mad-as-a-very-mad-fruitbat Mrs Merrill had just offered me a one-day try-out at her shop on Saturday…

Chapter 11

TOM HANKS? NO THANKS.

"You can't put *him* on your list! He's old! *And* he doesn't qualify!" Chloe barked at Jen.

It was only meant to be a laugh, a stupid game of list-making that filled an otherwise dull Wednesday-afternoon breaktime. But for once, Jen didn't giggle. She looked really offended that Chloe wouldn't let her have Tom Hanks (her favourite ever actor) on her Top-Five Totty list. But to be fair to Chloe, she *had* specified that the list had to be made up of boys we actually knew, or knew-ish. *And* they had to be boys. Forgive me for being pernickety, but as Tom Hanks doesn't live in Crouch End, London, N8 and he's several decades older than any boy we know, he didn't qualify on either count.

"Well, I can only think of four people round here that I fancy – so why can't I put Tom Hanks on to make it up to five?" Jen protested.

"Because he's disgusting," Chloe said flatly, putting a blunt end to Jen's argument.

"Yewww…" shuddered Kellie. "I don't know how you can fancy him anyway, Jen – why can't you go for someone who's less than a hundred years old?"

"He was good in *Forrest Gump*, though," said Sandie, slithering away from my side and trying to show some solidarity to Jen, who was looking seriously wobbly now that someone had dared to have a dig at her ultimate Hollywood human.

"Yeah, but plenty of actors are good in films – it doesn't mean you have to get a crush on them," Salma blinked slowly at Jen and Sandie. "Specially when they're as minging as Tom Hanks…"

While my friends were debating just how "minging" Tom Hanks was or wasn't, I found myself staring at my own Top-Five Totty list, which the girls had all been teasing me about right before Chloe started on Jen.

So, I'd written down Alfie's name five times. So what?

Quickly, I scrunched the list up and aimed it right at the bin. The last thing I needed was to have it flutter out of my pocket at home, only to be discovered by Linn. I've done a stunning job so far of hiding the fact that I have a crush the size of France on her best friend, but – and I might be wrong here – a list headed "Ally's Top-Five Totty" followed by "Alfie!" x 5, and with loveheart doodles all around it might *just* give the game away.

But my perfectly projected ping! missed its mark. Or at least, the flight path of my scrunched note was interrupted – instead of landing in the bin, it boinged off the side of a passing teacher's head and rolled right under a radiator.

"Sorry!" I cringed, as Mrs Wilson from the English department gave me the evil eye.

She threw me the sort of do-that-again-and-it's-detention dirty look that teachers specialize in, and carried on walking. For about half a second.

Omigod, she'd stopped. Omigod, she was turning round. Omigod, it looked like she'd decided not to let me off with just the regulation dirty-look thing after all.

"You're Ally Love, aren't you?" she said, holding her plastic folder and pen clenched tight to her chest.

"Yuh-hung…"

It's hard to get words to do the right thing when you're about to be charged with assaulting a teacher with a lethal paper-ball and all your friends are watching open-mouthed.

"So, how's your sister?"

I hadn't been prepared for that. If Mrs Wilson had said, "Get to the Headmaster's office NOW!"

or "That's it – you've got detention till you're 35!" or something, then I wouldn't have been so shocked. Mortified, maybe, but not shocked.

"Which one?" I asked, trying frantically to remember whether it was Linn or Rowan who had the (dis)pleasure of being taught by Mrs Wilson.

"Rowan," she replied.

The wind whistled through my empty, clueless head. What was the silly old bat asking about Rowan for?

"She wasn't in class this afternoon?" said Mrs Wilson, giving me a huge hint.

"Ahhhh…" I mumbled in a long, drawn-out breath, to give myself time to think.

Mrs Wilson stared hard at my gently reddening face, waiting for a response. To one side of me, I could practically *hear* the silence as my mates held their breath.

"Rowan … is … I mean, *has*…"

The corner of my mouth started to vibrate as the lie began to form.

"…diarrhoea!" I finally exclaimed.

"Mmm," muttered Mrs Wilson, narrowing her eyes and believing me not one bit.

Which was fair enough since it was a big, fat lie.

"Tell her to get better soon, then."

"I will," I nodded at Mrs Wilson.

I'll tell her, all right, I thought to myself. *I'll tell her right after I've killed her for making me cover for her like this…*

Chapter 12

NUH-UH...

OK, so when Mrs Wilson corralled me in the corridor, my first reaction was to suspect Rowan was skiving.

But then, as soon as I'd parked my bum on the uncomfortable stool in the science class, my highly attuned Worrying Gland kicked in.

And my pattern of worrying went like this...

Stage 1. *Why would Rowan skive off? She's never done it before, as far as I know.*

Stage 2. *She's dead!*

Stage 3. *Stop it – she's* not *dead. She was making herself a tuna and pea sandwich when I went home at lunchtime (blee). And she left for school a couple of minutes before me, so if she'd been run over by a rampaging milk float or something, I'd have come across her lying in the gutter, covered in semi-skimmed.*

Stage 4: *Aaargh! But she could have been abducted – it can happen so fast; one minute you're there and the next you're gone...*

Stage 5: *I've got to ask Miss Kyriacou if I can leave class, so I can go and tell someone that my sister's been abducted!*

Stage 6: *But what if I tell people Rowan's been abducted, and she really is just skiving? I'll get her into terrible trouble...*

Stage 7: *But what if I keep my mouth shut, and she really has been abducted?*

Stage 8: *Don't panic – she hasn't been abducted. She's just skiving. I hope.*

Stage 9: *Return to Stage 1, and repeat for two lessons and the entire walk home after school...*

By the time I got to my front door, I had an ulcer. Well, not a proper one, but a serious burny, churny knot. And it was burning, churning and knotting because I had convinced myself that I'd open the front door and find my whole family weeping and wailing over my poor squashed-in-the-road/abducted sister.

But instead, there was the sound of giggling, shooing and cooing...

In order of appearance – as I followed the sounds and bumbled through to the kitchen – there was Tor (doing the giggling), Grandma (with a tea towel in her hand, doing the shooing) and Britney the pigeon (doing the cooing. And the pooing, actually – right on the kitchen floor).

"Tor, dear, stop laughing and help me get this bird out of the house, please!" ordered Grandma, staring sternly from the small, smirking boy to the puzzled-looking pigeon flapping around on the table.

Britney is a fairly recent addition to our house-cum-zoo. Tor found her, battered, bruised and dragging her poorly pigeon wing about, when we were at Camden Market a couple of months back. He took her home to recuperate, and after regaining her strength and unruffling her feathers in our garden shed, Tor held a very dramatic release ceremony, which was compulsory for all of us in the family to attend, as well as a few of his buddies from school.

But the release wasn't as dramatic as we'd expected: after Tor had come out of the shed and launched Britney skyward (with lots of accompanying "Ooh!"s from us lot), she'd promptly fluttered into the nearest tree, and has stayed there ever since. Except, of course, when she's down on the bird table, eating the nuts and old bread that Tor sticks out for her every day. Or when she's got impatient for her waiter to bring her her tea and has flapped her way through the open back door to see what the hold-up is in the kitchen...

As I watched Tor try to tempt Britney out of

the door by wafting a Jaffa Cake under her beak, it suddenly occurred to me to ask for any sightings of my elusive sister.

"Hey, have you two seen—"

"Hello! I'm home!" I heard a voice interrupt me from the hallway.

There was a bang as the front door slammed shut, and a familiar *flippety-flap* as Rowan tripped up the stairs.

She wasn't getting away that easily...

Turning away from the bird-baiting drama in the kitchen, I went out into the hallway and thundered up behind Rowan, determined to find out what drama was going on with her.

"Where have you been?" I blurted out, barging into her fairy-light-lit room without bothering to knock. (Not nice, I know – but then I was still pretty wound up. Even if I was stupendously glad to see that she hadn't been abducted. Well, not bodily anyway. But what she said next made me wonder if her *brain* had been abducted and left a stupid great hole where it should have been...)

"What?" she asked me, her cheeks doing that pink hot-spot thing.

"Where have you been, Ro?" I repeated, trying to look stern, even though Rolf had just headbutted me in the knees as he squeezed his way into the room to see what all the excitement was about.

"What do you mean, 'Where have I been?' I've been at school, same as you!"

"Nuh-*uh!*"

OK, so "nuh-*uh*" isn't the smartest bit of cross-examining, but I had used up so much brainpower stressing out about Rowan all afternoon that I couldn't rely on my words to work.

Still, who was she kidding?

"Ro, if you were at school this afternoon, how come your teacher, Mrs Wilson, gave me a hard time, asking me why you weren't in her class? Hmm?"

Rowan's cheeks went as pinky-red as the roses on her white duvet. Her eyes were as wide as her mouth was open. She knew she'd been rumbled.

"But I ... I ... I *was* in her class today!" she stammered.

"What – but you just happened to be *invisible*?" I suggested sarcastically.

I mean, how dumb did she think I was? Or Mrs Wilson for that matter. Who could miss Rowan in a hurry? Even today, when she was dressed down again, she was still more noticeable than Harrods at Christmas, when the entire building is covered in white lightbulbs. It wasn't that Rowan was her usual colourful self today (hair scraped back and dressed in mostly black again, I noticed, except for the return of the red velvet mules). It was just that she was tinkling. Yeah – tinkling. Rolf had noticed it too; he was jerking his head round every time he heard it, as if he was expecting Colin or one of the other cats to emerge in their belled collars at any second.

"Where's that tinkling noise coming from?" I quizzed her.

Reluctantly, Rowan pulled up her school shirt and showed me. It was a belly chain made out of a fine strip of black leather, with teeny-tiny silver balls attached every few centimetres.

"Do you like it?" Rowan asked, batting her long, dark lashes at me appealingly.

(Right that second she reminded me of a goofy-but-sweet King Charles spaniel that me and the dogs often meet up in Ally Pally park at the weekend. I looked at Rolf and really wished he could talk; just so I could ask him if he agreed with me.)

My honest answer about the belly chain? Well, it would have looked nice on a beach in Brazil, worn with a bikini, and preferably if you were a tanned-tummied goddess. But if I was honest, under a school uniform, in a crumbly terraced house in Crouch End, north London, and on a white-as-cottage-cheese stomach it looked a bit strange. Still, "strange" and "Rowan" kind of go hand-in-hand…

"It's … nice!" I said irritably. "But what happened to you today at school, Ro?"

If she tried to tell me she was there again, I'd scream. Or grab her by her belly chain and shake her till she played "Jingle Bells".

"I… I…"

Suddenly Rowan seemed all small and pathetic, as she flopped down on to her bed. Against the backdrop of the multi-coloured fairy lights twinkling round most things that stand still in her room, Rowan – with her dark hair, pale skin and big brown eyes – looked like a forlorn little pixie. And I was the big, bad, bullying witch, even though here I was, her thirteen-year-old kid sister.

I wasn't going to give in, though. She'd made me too sick with worry all afternoon to back down. I took a leaf out of Mrs Wilson's book and narrowed my eyes at her. It soon did the trick. (Thank you, Mrs Wilson, even if I do think you're a miserable old bat.)

"Please don't tell on me but I was at Von's she had the afternoon off college and begged me to come round and hang out with her I know it was stupid I won't do it again please don't tell Dad Ally please

107

please don't," blabbed Rowan in one breathless blur.

I'm not very good at confrontation. In fact, doing anything confrontational gives me the same twitchy thing as lying does. But while I'd got Rowan talking at last, I had to hit her with the stuff Billy had said.

"Ro," I began tentatively, feeling one shoulder go a bit juddery, "someone I know saw you on Saturday night up at Muswell Hill Broadway. Bil— I mean, he— I mean, this person saw you staggering about, like you were drunk. Or something."

"What? Billy saw me and thought I was *drunk*?! How *could* he?!" Rowan gasped.

Oh wow. I wish I hadn't started this now. And so much for me "subtly" keeping Billy's identity under cover.

"I wasn't drunk, Al!" whimpered Rowan.

Rolf immediately stopped searching for non-existent cats and their tinkling collars and started gently whining in sympathy.

"But, Billy said you were sort of … *staggering* and stuff!" I tried to argue, feeling horrible now that Rowan looked so hurt.

"We were just being silly! Goofing around!" she whimpered again.

Whiiiinnnnnnne!!

"Shush, Rolf," I said soothingly, patting him on his big, hairy head.

"Chazza just kept pushing me off the pavement, for a laugh! Honest!" Rowan tried to explain in a high-pitched, pleading squeak.

Aaa-oooooooooooowwww!

Right – enough was enough. Either Rowan was going to start crying or Rolf was going to start howling at the moon (or both) and my jangled nerves couldn't stand it.

I had to get back to normality. Even if that was a kitchen full of grumpy grannies, Jaffa Cakes and flapping pigeons.

"I'm going to make some tea. Do you want a cup?" I said softly, grabbing an agitated Rolf by the collar and hauling him out of the room.

"Yes, please," sniffed Rowan, managing a swift, wobbly smile.

"Jaffa Cake?" I added.

"Yes, please," nodded Rowan.

Well, in her delicate state, she'd never notice the odd peck-mark or two...

Chapter 13

TO SKIRT OR NOT TO SKIRT...

"What's wrong with your black cords?" Sandie whispered.

She had to whisper. Teachers don't really like you discussing what you're going to wear for your try-out Saturday job. In fact, they don't like to hear you discussing clothes when they're teaching you full stop. Funny, that...

"I dunno," I shrugged in reply, while looking down at my legs under the desk.

There were a couple of dusty paw-prints on my thigh, I noticed. Cat-sized.

By the way, it wasn't just me and Sandie that were doing the whispering. Everyone was beginning to witter away, seeing as Mr Horace was a bit distracted. He was tutting a lot and trying to get the TV to work, so that we could all enjoy the treat of *Maths is Fun! No – We're Not Just Paid To Say That!* or whatever. (Now, I'm no electrical engineer, but if I was brave enough – and if I cared enough – I might have been tempted to point out to Mr Horace that thumping a badly behaved TV repeatedly on its side with your fist is liable to cause even *more* damage to it.) Still, at least Mr Horace's mistreatment of the telly gave me a few seconds' cover to continue my conversation with Sandie.

"But they're really nice trousers. *And* they look smart enough without being ... y'know – *smart*," Sandie hissed helpfully.

"Yeah," I shrugged again, while spitting on my finger and rubbing away the paw-prints.

Dad had bought me these cords to wear to school a couple of months ago.

And *that* was the problem.

"It's just that they make me feel ... thirteen," I mumbled, knowing it was pathetic.

But just their association with school and the fact that they had this little "Age 12–13" tag sewn in the waistband made me come over all under age again. Not, by the way, that I assumed Mrs Merrill would be inspecting the inside of my trousers when I stepped into her shop in a couple of days time (I think that's an arrestable offence, actually). But, unlike my immaculate sister Linn, I find it very hard to stop my clothes from a) having a magnetic attraction to pet hairs and b) staying where I want them to. This means that socks slither down, tops ride up and tags ping out on a regular basis. And Mrs Merrill might be mad and wear a wig, but I'm pretty sure she can read OK – specially a sticky-out tag that says "Age 12–13".

"What about your combats?" Sandie suggested next.

"Too laid-back," I shook my head.

"Your jeans?"

"Too scruffy."

"Your purple velvet trousers?"

"Too clubby."

"What about a skirt"

"Too … skirty," I shuddered.

The thing about skirts is that I really like them. On other people. And on hangers in shops. It's like, I see a cute-looking skirt, so I'll try it on. And it'll look kind of OK, but within about half a second, I just really want to get into a pair of kecks again. I don't know why; maybe I'm just allergic to skirts.

"Well, why don't I come round tomorrow night and we'll do a dress rehearsal?" said Sandie.

I was just about to tell her that that was a fantastic idea, and that she should maybe bring around her new charcoal-grey trousers from TopShop, just in case they suited me, when we were rudely interrupted.

"What are you two doing tomorrow night?"

asked Kyra, slithering herself right across her desk behind us and joining in the conversation.

"Are you earwigging?" I teased her.

"Well, I wouldn't *have* to if you two *spoke* properly, instead of whispering," she grinned at me, not even attempting to lower her voice. "So what are we doing tomorrow evening, girls?"

I didn't mind that she'd invited herself. The more the merrier – and it would take my mind off my try-out on Saturday: i.e. distract me from barfing through sheer nerves.

"Dress rehearsal – I'm working out what to wear for my first day at the card shop."

First day … last day. Who knew how it was going to turn out? Oh God, I was starting to feel a bit sick already.

"Great – I'll bring some of my stuff, if you want to borrow something," said Kyra breezily. "But if I was you, the one thing I'd definitely wear is a pair of headphones and a Walkman. You are going to get *sooo* bored!"

She did one of her throaty cackles. It was so loud I wouldn't have been surprised if Linn had heard it reverberating over in the sixth-form block.

"Shush, he'll hear you, Kyra!" warned Sandie, her enormo-blue eyes wide and round as headlights.

"Who? Horse-arse?" she replied, with a "so-what?"

expression on her face. "He's too busy faffing with the telly!"

"Not too busy to give you detention tonight, Kyra Davies!" came a booming male voice from the front of the class.

As Kyra sighed and grumpily slithered back into her seat, me and Sandie faced forward smartish and tried *very* hard to look like we didn't know her...

"Sorry..." I muttered, from the discomfort of one of the school loos.

"No worries," Kyra yawned from outside the cubicle somewhere.

I don't know why I felt the need to say sorry to her in the first place – Kyra hadn't got detention just 'cause she had been talking to me and Sandie (if that was the case, the whole class would have got detention, since everyone was blah-blahing quite happily while Mr Horace broke the TV some more). It's just that calling Mr Horace "Horse-arse" in a very loud, very sarky voice is kind of asking for it. And Kyra did that all by herself.

Reaching over for some loo roll, I saw that – surprise, surprise – there was none. (That's not including the full, soggy roll that was sitting in an ominous puddle on the floor...)

"Hey, Kyra, Sandie – can one of you do me a favour?" I called out to my mates. "Can you chuck me some loo paper under the door?"

"Sure!" I heard Sandie say. The other thing I heard was the flick-flicking of some magazine pages, so it looked like Kyra wasn't exactly joining in the hunt.

"None in here ... uh – none in there either," Sandie kept up a running commentary as she banged open every free cubicle door. "Aww – yuck! How can anybody be so disgusting?"

While Sandie was playing loo inspector, I sat slouched where I was, with my feet on tiptoes to avoid the dubious puddle, grumbling to myself about how much hassle it was to go for a simple wee in our scuzzy school toilets.

Then, just as I was mulling over that (disgusting) thought, my eyes settled on something scribbled on the back of the cubicle door. It was right at the end of this really boring, long piece of graffiti that's been going for a couple of months; graffiti that had started out with someone writing *"Ellie F is a total muppet"*, then someone underneath added *"I know who you are, and YOU are the muppet!"*, then in completely different handwriting, there was *"No, you are the muppet, you big MUPPET!"*, and it went on and on and *on* like that.

But now there was a new addition to the slagging.

Who's getting it this time? I wondered, bending forward to make out the red-penned scrawl.

Then I wished I hadn't bothered.

"The biggest Muppit at Pallace Gates", wrote someone who couldn't write, *"is Rowen Love"*.

Unless a new girl with a ridiculously similar name – give or take the odd vowel – had started at our school, then it looked like my sister had just been voted this week's muppet.

Uh-oh...

Chapter 14

TARAMASALATA, ANYONE?

"Ro!" I called out, when I got home at lunchtime. "Ro! You home?"

It didn't look like it. Unless she'd transformed herself into a grumpy-looking, short, hairy dog carrying an old, curly-edged Odour-Eater between her clenched teeth.

"Winslet? Where's Rowan? Hmm?" I bent forward and asked, hoping our number two hound would turn into a search-and-rescue dog or anything else remotely useful for once. "Fetch! Fetch her, Winslet!"

Winslet gave me a withering look then bounded off up the stairs, in search of a dark and dusty corner to hide her latest treasure.

"What about you, Rolfy?" I said, ruffling the head of our number one hound, who'd just padded out of the living room, yawning, after an energetic morning shedding hairs all over the sofa.

He licked my hand, then, sensing there wasn't a sandwich in it yet, he tippetty-tapped his way over the polished (and scuffed) hall floor towards the kitchen.

"OK, I get the message," I mumbled, hanging up my blazer and following him through. "So, what do you fancy? Low-fat strawberry yogurt? Cottage cheese with chives? Taramasalata? Whatever that is?"

I was pointing to everything in the fridge that had those annoying "Property of Linn Love" Post-It notes stuck on. I mean, when is Linn going to give up doing that? She seems to think that it'll put me and Rowan off nicking any of her "special" stuff, but it just has totally the opposite effect.

"Is Rowan skiving again?" I asked Rolf, who was happily licking the gloopy taramasalata stuff off the finger I was holding out to him.

I knew, without anyone (any *dog*) answering, that she was. Skiving, I mean. But what was I going to do about it? If I told Dad, it would just be another big hassle for him to sort out, just when he could probably do with a break. If I told Grandma, she'd be really disappointed with Ro, and give her some big lecture. If I told Linn, it would just be more ammunition for her; she'd treat Rowan like she's (even more of) a goofball. If I told Tor, he'd just get quietly worried and ask if a visit to the zoo might make Rowan feel better.

OK, so I knew I wanted to try to help Rowan (of course I did – I had already spent a good few minutes that morning, doodling over the "Muppet" graffiti with Kyra's eyeliner pencil so that no-one else could read it. And if *that* isn't being a good sister I don't know what is (especially since it meant that I owed Kyra a new eyeliner pencil). I also knew that I wanted Rowan to get into as little trouble as possible, which meant sorting this out on my own...

Von's number is in the address book that lives beside the phone in the hall. Dad's got the number of all our friends in there, so that *if* he ever worries about where we are or what we're doing, he can reach us. Not that he's ever done it – it's more like an insurance policy, I guess.

While I listened to the phone ring, I could hear a whirring coming from upstairs, where one of Tor's small furballs was running a marathon in its metal wheel. The whirring was going as fast as the whirring in my mind – I was trying very quickly to think of the right thing to say, if anyone ever bothered to pick up the phone, that was.

After ten thousand rings and a seventeen-year wait, I was just about to give up and stick the receiver back down when the phone was finally answered.

"Hello?"

It was Von. And it was just a wild guess (fnar), but if she was answering the phone, then it meant she wasn't at college. Which meant Rowan was very probably there. Again.

"Von? It's Ally," I squeaked.

"Who?"

I've only known Von for like *two years*, and she has to ask me who I am. But then, when I say I know her, I use the term very loosely. Whenever Von comes round to our house, she's always pretty polite and everything to my dad and Grandma, and she's really nice to Tor (mainly 'cause he's as much of a space cadet as Rowan is, in his own way). But when it comes to me and Linn, forget it. Von doesn't think much of Linn at all – Rowan once told *me* that Von told *her* Linn's way too uptight and straight. And me? I think I'm just too boring for her to bother with. I'm thirteen, I don't have weird dress sense, I don't have any interesting character hang-ups (championship worrying doesn't count), and I have no random bits of me pierced or tattooed.

And you know something? It's kind of tough knowing that you rate really low in someone else's consciousness. Specially when I'm totally fascinated by Von. Who wouldn't be? She's totally like

Morticia Addams, except with black combats and a nose stud.

"Ally," I repeated my name. "Rowan's sister?"

"Oh yeah..." Von replied.

And then didn't say anything else.

"Uh, is she there?"

I heard the phone clunk down and could only suppose that Von had gone to get my missing sister. Or maybe I'd just bored her so much with my dull, thirteen-year-old normal-ness that she'd just dozed off on the spot or something.

"Ally?"

Good – it was Rowan.

"Ro!" I exclaimed, relieved that I'd tracked her down.

"What are you doing phoning here, Al?" said Rowan, sounding distinctly huffy around the edges.

Well, pardon me, I thought, feeling equally huffy. *I was only concerned.*

"Why aren't you here?" I said instead.

"Because I'm *here*!" said Rowan defensively.

This was turning out to be a stupid conversation. And she was making me feel stupid for trying to help.

"You didn't go into school this morning, did you?" I blurted out.

I didn't know that for sure – it was only a guess. But Rowan didn't seem in a hurry to deny it.

"That's none of your business, Ally!" Rowan snapped.

I felt my face flush. Rowan didn't snap at me – ever.

"Ro, if Mrs Wilson or any of your other teachers ask me where you are, I'm not going to cover for you again!" I announced, feeling a bit shaky round the edges.

"Fine!" said Rowan, before slamming the phone down on me.

Right – that was it. I didn't care if my in-between, weirdo sister got into trouble.

And I had half a mind to go back into the school loos this afternoon and wipe off Kyra's eyeliner – so the world could see that Rowan Love really *was* a muppet, thank you very much…

Chapter 15

SYMPATHY AND SNAKES

I was totally miserable all afternoon after my fight with Rowan.

OK, so technically, it wasn't *really* a fight – more like a big, spiky huff – but it was as close as me and Rowan had ever got to a fight.

In fact, I was *so* miserable that right after school, Sandie did something that made me cry. (Before you go thinking that Sandie had a personality transplant and turned from being the sweetest mate anyone could have into Cruella De Vil, I'll explain…)

I was supposed to be going to Billy's house straight after school; he'd phoned the night before (Wednesday) asking me to come round and and help him with his Maths homework (tonight, Thursday). It just shows how bad Billy is at Maths, when he has to ask *me* – who got twenty-seven per cent in my last-but-one Maths test – to help *him*.

Anyway, come four o'clock and home-time, I was planning on just mumbling "bye" to Sandie and moping my way over to the W3 bus stop, where I could catch a bus that would take me over the hill, past Ally Pally, and on to Billy's place. But Sandie persuaded me to hang on for a couple of minutes, asking me to come over to the shops with her and wait while she went into the mini-supermarket for a magazine/some chewing gum/a dead mouse/some high-octane explosives or whatever else she'd told me that I hadn't heard (hadn't listened to, more like). So I was hovering in a generally miserable way when she came out and presented me with a chewy, marshmallowy snake sweet that was nearly as long as my arm.

"Thought you needed cheering up," she smiled, putting her head to one side and gazing sadly at me.

To be honest, I'd have preferred a Toblerone, or a Chunky Kit-Kat. But I was so touched by Sandie's thoughtfulness that I just stared stupidly at the snake as though it was the most special thing I'd ever been given in my life. Then she *really* did the wrong thing; she put her arm around me and said, "Don't worry, Ally Pally – it'll all be OK!"

And that's when I started blubbing.

That's the thing when you're feeling miserable and sorry for yourself, isn't it? All it takes is for one person be really nice and understanding and you end up doing an impression of Niagara Falls.

And, of course, right then – right when I'm having a soggy moment of weakness – over walk Salma and Jen.

"What's wrong?" asked Salma, as she and Jen stared hard at me, their expressions all alarmed and curious at the same time.

I mean, how could I tell them? I knew Sandie understood (as a best mate always does), but how could I stand there with a marshmallow snake in my hand and snot dripping out of my nose and tell Salma and Jen that this was all because I had a bit of a bust-up with my sister? It would sound *so* lame…

"She just tripped and hurt her arm," Sandie covered up for me. "She'll be OK – won't you, Ally?"

Good old dependable Sandie. I nodded a bit and rummaged through my pockets for something to mop up Niagara.

"Aww!" said Jen, beating me to it and handing me a white tissue she'd pulled from her bag.

I wished she hadn't bothered – from the blue ink-stain and unidentifiable crumbs and fluff attached to it, it had been in there for a long, *long* time. Still, it would have been rude to refuse it, so I parped my nose hard into it and hoped none of the crumbs and fluff would stick to my face.

"I don't think your sister's having too much luck this afternoon either," said Salma, gazing at me through her spookily long, dark eyelashes.

"Who, Linn?" I sniffed.

"No – Rowan," Salma replied. "We just saw her a couple of minutes ago by the water fountain, and she was having a really big argument or something with Lisa Dean and Tasha Franklin."

For a millisecond I was pleased – if Salma and Jen had seen Rowan, then it meant she'd come back to school in the afternoon, so even if I felt rotten, at least our bust-up made her think twice. And then my heart sank; what was Rowan arguing about? And what was she doing arguing with Lisa Dean and Tasha Franklin? They were only two of the toughest girls in Rowan's year; the kind of girls who think it's really funny to put stones in the middle of snowballs and spit chewing gum from the third floor stairwell just for the fun of seeing whose hair it lands in.

I'd kind of stopped crying as soon as Salma and Jen had turned up (embarrassment has a great drying-up effect), but hearing this stuff about Rowan really shook me out of blub-mode (panic too has a great drying-up effect).

"I'd better go and see what's going on," I muttered, starting to walk back in the direction of school.

"Nah – she's left already," said Jen. "We saw her running to catch the 144."

The 144 bus? The only time Rowan ever caught that was when she was going on one of her little after-school shopping trips to Wood Green. Was she going to splurge on something again? When we absolutely couldn't afford a single splurge?

Suddenly, a switch in my brain flipped from being worried about Rowan, to being mad with her again. This was turning into a bit of a habit...

I was *so* mad, I decided right there and then to walk up over the Palace to Billy's house. Stomping across the hill would help me to get rid of some aggression (i.e. I could spend twenty whole minutes picturing how I could *kill* my thoughtless sister) and save on the bus fare too.

Well, if one of the Love family was so busy chucking money away, then the least I could do was try to spend nothing.

Feeling virtuous and grumpy, I left Sandie and the others standing on the pavement while me and my snake stomped off...

"...and then it's just a case of multiplying *that*, by *that*," I explained, punching numbers into Billy's calculator.

"Uh-huh," I heard him mumble.

"Oh…" I muttered, blinking from the calculator to the page in the textbook and back again. "Er, maybe you're meant to *divide* it."

"Uh-huh," Billy mumbled again.

There I was, trying to make sense of stuff that made my head go twirly, and what was Billy doing? It took me a minute to twig, but the rustle of paper soon gave him away.

"Billy!" I yelped, turning round and catching him reading *Match* instead of looking at the Maths questions I was trying to help him with. (Probably just as well, really, since I hadn't the teensiest clue what I was doing…)

"Oh! Sorry!" grinned Billy, as if *Match* had just accidentally *materialized* in his hand.

"Look, I'm not here just for fun, you know!" I told him off.

But it wasn't true. Coming round to Billy's was always fun (apart from his stupid dog and his stuck-up mum, of course). Billy has this brilliant way of talking drivel that always made me laugh. *And* it's easy to wind him up and tease him, and I couldn't get away with that at home (Linn would tell me to get lost, Rowan wouldn't "get" it, and Tor's too sweet to wind up).

Even though I don't like her too much, it's quite

good fun to wind Billy's mum up too. I mean, I know she used to be a friend of Mum's once upon a time (though goodness knows why), and I know she's been really nice to Dad and got him to come along to hers and Billy's dad's evening class (I can hardly bring myself to say *line-dancing* class – good grief) but she's such a snob, she really is.

It was like at teatime, she starts showing off about Billy's big sister Beth and how well she's doing in her study year out in France ('scuse me, but this Beth that she's so proud of is the same one that's hardly ever bothered to get in touch with her entire family since she went to university). Anyhow, I couldn't resist it: I had to ask, "Where is Beth again, Mrs Stevenson?" It's not like I don't know that Beth is in Paris (who could forget the capital city of France?), but I just love it when she puffs up like a proud pigeon and says, "She's in Par*ee*!" in this naff French accent. And when I did it tonight, Billy didn't let me down – he got caught in a snort of laughter *just* when he'd eaten a mouthful of bolognese and did this *excellent* tomatoey nose spray over his mum's blindingly white tablecloth.

"Hold on," Billy said now, pointing back down to the cartoon he'd been reading in his mag when he was supposed to be listening to me get his homework wrong. "I just want to finish this page..."

"Nope!" I replied, yanking the magazine off his lap. "You've got to concentrate on *this*!"

"Ooooh!" Billy gasped, holding his hands up in front of him and pretending to be scared of me. "You're *such* a bully, Ally Love!"

And that's when it hit me – not the fact that I will never, *ever* be any good at Maths, no matter *how* hard I try, but the thing about bullying.

Rowan acting tetchy recently... Rowan skiving school... Rowan and the chewing gum on her blazer... Rowan running that day when I heard someone yelling horrible stuff... Rowan looking all upset when I saw her with Von afterwards... Rowan looking gutted holding on to those broken heart-shaped sunglasses... Rowan and the graffiti... Rowan arguing in the playground this afternoon...

Were Lisa Dean and Tasha Franklin bullying my sister?

Chapter 16

"G" IS FOR...

I didn't stay long at Billy's after that. Once that thing about bullying and Rowan had weasled its way into my head, I couldn't get it out.

Billy seemed sort of disappointed when I said I was going home. He even tried to distract me by doing this impersonation of his Maths teacher, Mr Murphy, but since I don't go to Billy's school and don't *know* Mr Murphy it was hard to be too excited by it. Specially since Billy's impersonation was just made up of Billy doing a stupid walk and talking in a voice that was Billy's, only a bit deeper.

When I got home, I peered round into the living room but, although the telly was on, there was no-one there – unless you count four cats (one that was Colin and three that weren't) and Winslet, who'd fallen asleep on the mat while chewing a toothbrush. It was too chewed up to make out whose toothbrush it was (well, it was safe to say it was Winslet's now...).

I could hear the gush of water coming from the tap in the kitchen (and the gurgle and thud of water pipes juddering the length of the house because of it), so I walked through, catching sight of my dad at the sink.

"What are you doing?" I asked him, thinking it was pretty late to be tackling the dishes, especially since we all do them in a rota right after tea (I should have been on drying duty tonight, but I'd been round at Billy's watching him pebble-dash the table with bolognese).

"Oh, hi, Ally Pally!" my dad grinned, looking over his shoulder at me. "I didn't expect you back so soon. I thought you were Linn for a second – she's out somewhere or other tonight."

He was holding a blazer, I noticed. For a second, I wondered if it was mine, and then I realized I still had my uniform on (duh).

"I was just coming back down from putting Tor to bed when I spotted Rowan's jacket on the coat rack," he explained, holding the jacket up.

Uh-oh, I thought. *More chewing gum?*

"There's some sort of chalky marks on the back of it," Dad continued. "Dunno what she's been up to, but I just thought I'd sponge them off…"

"Where is Ro?" I asked him, feeling my thudding heart slide up from my chest and into my mouth.

Should I tell him? I fretted. *Should I just blurt out what I think? Or should I speak to Rowan first?*

"She's gone to bed. Bad headache, she said."

My mouth was just about to open, ready to spill, when Dad spoke again.

"You don't think Rowan's stressing out about the money situation, do you?" he asked me.

I noticed that his short, dark, spiky hair was coming together like a point at the front. It looked funny – like an exclamation mark. Only his face spoilt it – all concerned and worried and tense.

"I don't think it's that..." I shook my head, as I wandered over to the sink and stood beside him.

At that second, a vision of Rowan flitted through my mind; a vision of Ro leaping on to the 144 to Wood Green in search of trinkets and baubles to cheer herself up after a long, hard afternoon being bullied by Lisa Dean and Tasha Franklin.

"'Cause you girls shouldn't worry yourselves," said Dad, staring at me with serious brown eyes that told me *he* was still busy doing any worrying that had to be done. "And it's lovely of you to try and get this Saturday job, Ally, but you don't have to do it. I'm sure we'll be out of this bad patch pretty soon..."

On the one hand I felt reassured by what he'd just said – but only the bit about my Saturday job.

It just meant that he hadn't realized yet that I was, strictly speaking, too young to do it. But the "I'm sure we'll be out of this bad patch pretty soon..." stuff didn't exactly make me feel too fantastic.

Should I tell him? Should I not...? I mused at a million kilometres an hour.

"Dad, I, um, I—"

But I didn't get any further than that, thanks to a small, practically inaudible cry, followed by Rolf coming skittering into the kitchen anxiously, his four paws sliding over the lino in his haste to alert us to the fact that Tor was having a bad dream.

"Uh-oh," said Dad, staring upwards, as if he had X-ray vision that could pierce the kitchen roof and let him see straight into Tor's room up on the first floor.

"Here, I'll do that," I said, grabbing the jacket and the soggy sponge out of Dad's hands.

"Thanks, Ally Pally – better see how the little guy's doing," Dad smiled gratefully, bounding out of the kitchen and following Rolf into the hall.

I listened to six feet thundering up the stairs (two belonging to my dad, four belonging to Rolf) and then turned my attention to Rowan's blazer, holding it stretched out tight by the shoulders.

"G" was the first chalky letter.

The next was "E".

The one after was an "E" too.

Then "K", which all together spelt "GEEK".

OK, so if I'd had any doubts before I didn't have them now. 'Cause it sure wasn't the fairies that had scrawled that stuff on Rowan's jacket.

Chapter 17

WHO NEEDS MOUSSE WHEN YOU'VE GOT MARMALADE?

I didn't get a chance to have a private talk with Dad for the rest of the evening, mainly 'cause poor little Tor was fretty and miserable and too scared to fall asleep in case his bad dream came back.

In the end, I went to bed. Dad – and Tor – eventually nodded off in front of some snoresville political programme (I think it was so dull that it zonked them out like a sleeping pill). Linn gently shook Dad awake when she got home, and he took Tor up to his room.

But Tor's bad dreams had started up the minute he got put back in his own bed, and the only thing that would calm him down was Dad lying down beside him till he fell asleep again. It worked OK, only Dad woke up at half past six in the morning on the floor of Tor's room, where he'd rolled at some point in the night. Tor, meanwhile, had tiptoed up to my room in the wee, small hours – I discovered him when the alarm went off, all curled up with Colin under the duvet at the bottom of the bed.

Now Dad was sitting at the kitchen table looking like he'd had a fight with a steamroller and lost.

"What exactly were you dreaming about last night, Tor?" I asked him, taking my place at the breakfast table with my brother, Dad and Linn.

"Dunno," shrugged Tor, quite happily, while biting the head off the toast bat he'd just carved.

"He can't remember," Linn continued, rolling her eyes at me.

All that drama and he'd totally forgotten it.

Dad made a little groaning noise and tried (and failed) to straighten his neck. But the hours of lying in a weird shape on a cold floor had taken their toll. It didn't look like this morning was a good time to talk to him either.

Plus, there wouldn't be time. We'd all have to leave for school soon, and I planned on breaking the habit of a lifetime and keeping Rowan company on the way there, so I could talk this bullying thing through with her.

(I had put my head around her bedroom door the night before, in the hope that she'd be awake. But her room had been in darkness – not the weeniest twinkle of a solitary fairy light – and Rowan was just a huddle under her rose-covered white duvet.)

"Where's Ro? Is she in the shower?" I asked anyone who cared to answer.

"No," Dad replied, grimacing and rubbing his neck with one hand. "She's off to the doctor's. She says she still got this headache and that she's been getting a lot of them lately."

"No wonder, since she sits in that stupid room of hers so much. That pink she painted her walls is enough to give *anyone* a migraine," interrupted Linn, as she licked some low-fat strawberry yoghurt (property of Linn Love) off her spoon.

I suddenly remembered that I'd eaten half of that yoghurt yesterday lunchtime, with a little help from Rolf, and now I was quite glad I had. I even quite hoped Rolf had left the odd doggy hair in it. Why did Linn always have to be so mean about Rowan?

"Anyway," Dad continued, shooting a bit of a tsk-tsk look Linn's way. "I told Rowan that she should go round to the surgery before school and try and get seen, or at least make an appointment for later."

She's getting those headaches because of the bullying! I've got *to tell him*, I thought, deciding that I'd wait till Linn had mooched off to school (after that last unsympathetic remark, I didn't want her knowing what was going on). Then I'd distract Tor by telling him I thought I could hear one of his stick insects whimpering or something, and he'd be off like a shot, leaving Dad to me.

Good plan.

Which – naturally – didn't work.

"Come on, Tor! We'll have to get going now; I've got to get round and open up the shop early today for a delivery of gear levers!" said Dad, rolling down the sleeves of his checked shirt as he got up from the table.

"Hold on – I'll help you out," Linn chipped in, getting to her feet too.

Rats – so much for getting Dad on his own.

I waved bye as Dad and Tor trundled out of the kitchen, then let my eyes fall on Miss Perfection, who was busy giving her perfection one final check in the mirror by the door, reaching up with her hands and smoothing down her already smooth, shiny, blondey hair.

Unconsciously copying her, I found myself running my fingers through my dull, brown hair, leaving a fine trail of toast crumbs and marmalade – which I wouldn't notice till I spotted my reflection in the school loos at breaktime…

"Why didn't you tell me?" I said into the mirror.

"I didn't notice!" Sandie protested, leaning in and staring at my reflection.

How could she not notice that half my breakfast

was in my hair? I mean, what are best friends for if it isn't to tell you when you're accidentally wearing toast and marmalade?

"Honestly, you can hardly see it…" Sandie tried to console me, as I carried on picking bits out.

"Yes you can!" grinned Kyra, leaning in from the other side. "Look! It's all over the place!"

I know Kyra was only being honest. But suddenly, I much preferred Sandie and her nice, comforting white lie.

"I forgot to put my brush in my bag this morning," I grumbled, pinging an especially big dollop of marmalade into the sink. "Could I borrow a brush or comb from one of you? It might get rid of this stuff quicker…"

"Get lost!" snorted Kyra. "I don't want *my* comb messed up with all that gloop!"

"There you go, Ally!" said Sandie, pulling out her Barbie hairbrush and passing it over to me.

Urgh. Barbie.

"You know, Kyra's right – it's not fair to mess up your brush. Look it's nearly all out, anyway!" I smiled at Sandie.

(And the translation of that is: "*Actually, I'd rather wander about with food in my hair than be seen by everyone in the school loos, using a brush with* Barbie *on it. And while I'm at it, why do your parents insist on buying you such totally corny stuff?!"*)

Then another face came into view behind me in the mirror.

"Rowan!" I squeaked, feeling stupidly surprised to see my own sister, at the school we both go to practically every day of our lives. (I say practically, to take into account weekends, holidays, and days when Rowan is skiving round at Von's...)

But I guess I was on edge with her; it was as if there was a big, unspoken secret between us. Actually, there *was* a big, unspoken secret between us, come to think of it.

I was just about to ask Rowan if she was all right and if she'd been to the doctor, when she spoke first.

"You know something, Ally, you *really* embarrassed me, yesterday!" she snapped at me, her brown eyes all dark in her whiter-than-white tense face. "I mean, phoning Von's like that, as if you were my mum or something!"

That wasn't a great thing to compare me to, since neither of us can hardly remember what our mum's voice is like *normally* never mind over the phone.

"Who do you think you are, ordering me back to school like that?" she snapped some more.

I didn't need to check in the mirror to know that my face was by now flushing prawn-pink. Normally, Rowan is such a funny little space cadet that I feel like *I'm her* big sister, and not the other way around. But here she was, telling me off worse than *Linn* ever had, and making me feel about three years old. *And* in front of my mates too.

I noticed that Rowan's hand was kind of shaking when she lifted it up and pointed her finger at me. God, she must have been *so* mad at me.

"Just leave me alone, OK, Ally?!"

OK, *I'll leave you alone*, I thought, trying hard not to go shaky myself. *I'll never care about you* or *worry about you again!*

For a second, I even imagined myself sneaking into her room and unscrewing one bulb from each of her string of fairy lights. (You only need to take one bulb out and *none* of them work. Sneaky, huh?)

"Wow!" gasped Kyra, as soon as Rowan had turned and flippety-flapped her way across the tiled floor and out of the loos. "I thought she was just weird! I didn't think she could do bitchy too!"

"Neither did I," I answered her, hoping my voice didn't sound as wobbly as I felt inside.

Sandie opened her mouth and closed it, then opened it again – stunned at seeing my kooky sister act like a complete dragon lady.

"Is Rowan all right?" asked Sandie, frowning so hard her eyebrows nearly met in the middle. "She doesn't look normal. I mean normal for *her*..."

It was true – once again, there was no mad hairdo, no wild clothes; only her little red embroidered mules made her stand out. Rowan looked (almost) like everyone else at school, and somehow, that didn't make sense.

"I don't really care," I shrugged, pretending to look in my bag for something that didn't exist.

(Translation: *I think I might cry, so I'm going to rummage around in my books for a minute until I get my tear ducts under control.*)

"Ally?!" a breathless voice suddenly blasted into my thoughts.

"I'm here!" I called out, raising my head and staring at Kellie, who'd just come barging through the door that lead out into the corridor.

"Thank goodness!" Kellie panted. "Chloe said she thought you were here!"

"Yeah, but why? What's up?" I asked her, with my heart squidging in and out in a panic.

"You've got to come quick – it's Rowan!"

I don't think I've ever moved so fast in my life.

I tell you, if I'd ever run that fast on a school sports day (fat chance), I'd have won a medal...

Chapter 18

HOW TO SHOCK BOYS, IN ONE EASY LESSON

If it hadn't been for the fact that Rowan was in the state she was in, it would have been quite funny.

A whole bunch of boys – some so startled that they hadn't done their flies up yet – were hovering about, stunned into stupidity at the sight of so many girls in their loos at once.

It had started with Lisa Dean and Tasha Franklin, who'd grabbed hold of Rowan about two seconds after she'd left me, and bundled her straight through the door with the *Boys* sign on it, straight past a load of flummoxed lads, and left her skidding in humiliation across the tiled floor.

Next, no sooner had Lisa and Tasha run out giggling, then I'd run in, followed by Kyra (who later told me she got quite a kick out of noseying about in there), Sandie (who hated it and was scared she'd pick up "boy germs", whatever *they* were), and Chloe and Kellie.

"She's in there!" said this one lad pointing towards a cubicle. "She just went in there and locked it!"

He didn't really need to tell me that – I could hear Rowan sniffling only too well. And over by the sinks, I could see the one red velvet shoe that she'd lost in the scuffle.

Poor Rowan; she was like Cinderella, huddled in the ashes. Although – and Sandie maybe had a point here – a bunch of ashes were probably a lot more hygienic than the smelly boys' toilets at Palace Gates school.

"Ro – it's me. Please open the door…" I said softly.

From behind the white cubicle door, the sniffling stopped. A bit.

"Go away!" said Rowan in a teeny-tiny voice.

"Please come out, Ro – Lisa and Tasha have gone now!"

At the mention of their names, Rowan did this sort of *whimper*, a bit like when Rolf goes to the vet and knows there's a needle with his name on waiting in the next room.

I looked around at my girlfriends, but they all pulled "uh-oh" faces and shrugged helplessly at me. Except for Kyra, who – bless her – started shooing all the boys out, even the ones who were a lot older than us.

"OK, Ro – you don't have to come out, but please open the door and let me come in," I tried to persuade her.

Me and the others all held our breath for a second, then heard a shuffle, followed by the screech of the lock being pulled back.

In the long, thin crack of the door, I could just make out Rowan's forlorn face – and quick as a flash, I slipped inside, before she changed her mind.

Rowan looked all crumpled and wet, but I think that was an optical illusion; she was huddled so far inside her blazer that it looked six sizes too big for her and she was mostly dry, apart from the big, fat tears scooting down her face and plopping off her jawline.

"Is it Lisa and Tasha?" I asked her, slithering my back down the door so that I ended up on my haunches in front of her. "Not just today, I mean – *all* of it."

Rowan nodded, and fluffy bits of brown hair started to come loose from the ponytail scrunchie at the nape of her neck.

"Is that why you've been acting so…"

I was going to say weird, but then that's Rowan's natural state, so I had to pick a better word.

"…*tense* about everything?"

She nodded again, and wiped her drippy nose with the back of her hand.

"Have they been giving you a really hard time?

Shouting at you and stuff?" I asked her, thinking of Monday, when I'd been on the way to my interview at Something Special and seen her running along the other side of the road.

"Yeah," she whispered. "It's 'cause of what I wear. They just go on and on and *on* at me, calling me names and stuff."

A soon as she said that, a thought walloped into my head.

"Those new sunglasses you had," I frowned at her, "did Lisa and Tasha break them?"

"Mmm-humm," she nodded shakily. "Tasha took them off me and Lisa stood on them. She said they were dumb."

Well, technically speaking, those purple, heart-shaped sunglasses *were* pretty dumb, but that was no reason to go standing on them. *I* think everything that presenter Ferne Cotton wears is dumb, but you don't see *me* hanging about outside TV studios, waiting to try to stand on her pink crocodile-skin cowboy boots. Or chuck her into boys' toilets.

"And you've been skiving off round at Von's, just to get away from them?"

Rowan nodded hard, so that more droplets of salty tears splashed around.

I was going to ask her about the chewing gum and chalked nastiness on her blazer, and about the graffiti in the girls' loos, but there didn't seem any point in going over all that stuff and upsetting her even more than she was already upset.

"Ally, that's the bell!" came a voice from floor level somewhere. I knew – you can hardly miss something that loud, even when you are in the middle of a family crisis.

"I'd better stay here," I told Sandie, who was peeking up at me from the small gap between the tiles and the cubicle door.

Another face appeared, as Kyra joined Sandie on the floor.

"We'll tell Mr Matthews that your sister was sick, and you had to take her home," said Kyra, coming over all enterprising.

"Do you want me to tell the office that you're ill, Rowan?" Sandie blinked up at my sister.

Rowan nodded down at her, tears welling in her eyes again.

"Thanks, guys," I whispered. "I'll take her home after everyone's gone to class and it's quiet."

I could make out the shuffle of a few footsteps as Sandie, Kyra, Chloe and Kellie made their way out, and then apart from the distant hubbub of passing people in the corridor, there was silence ... and Rowan's sniffling.

"We've got to tell someone, Rowan. We've got

to tell one of your teachers, and we've got to tell Dad!" I implored her.

"No!" she squeaked. "I can't tell Dad – he's too worried as it is! And I can't tell anyone at school! Li–Lisa an' Tasha said to me that if they got into trouble, they'd make things much, much worse for me!"

"But it's much worse already!" I tried to reason with her. "It was bad if they were just calling you names and stuff, but if they're breaking your things, and starting to shove you around..."

I was trying to sound like I knew what I was talking about, but inside my head was a big sign saying *Panic! Panic! Panic!* It's just that I knew what she meant – girls like Lisa and Tasha were seriously scary. Another thing I knew was that I didn't know what to do.

But I knew someone who would...

I don't know who designed the windows in the doors of the sixth-form block, but whoever it was was *really* tall.

I must have looked like a total moron, jumping up and down outside every classroom, desperately trying to peer in and catch a glimpse of Linn. All the while, Rowan was still locked away in her cubicle in the boys' toilets, going absolutely nowhere till

Linn and I came back for her and took her home.

And that's where we were now, the three of us sitting in the living room, at eleven-thirty on a Friday morning, while everyone else was in school.

It was nice – well as nice as it can be when you've just found out that your sister's being tortured by some brain-dead meatheads. It was nice because Rowan was lying on the sofa with her head in Linn's lap, while Linn gently stroked her head – just like Mum used to do when we were little – and tried to keep Rolf from licking Ro's face in sympathy.

And let me tell you, that doesn't happen too often in our house (Linn and Rowan being so close, I mean. Rolf licks everyone's face all the time, especially after he's just eaten his very honky Dog-E-Chunks or whatever).

"And Von and Chazza," said Linn, "do they know what's going on with you?"

"Only a little bit," Rowan replied, blinking up at her. "I told them some stuff when it all first started up, but they both wanted to come down and speak to Lisa and Tasha about it and warn them off, and I just thought that would make things a thousand times worse for me, so I stopped telling them anything."

"So, you've been keeping this stuff all to yourself?" asked Linn.

"Uh-huh. And it's just made me feel so *tense* and everything, like I've got to be looking over my shoulder all the time," Rowan went on. "I never feel like I can just, y'know, relax. And that's … that's kind of why I got out of it last Saturday."

"How do you mean?" asked Linn, gazing down at her.

"Well, I was out with Von and Chazza and everyone…"

As Rowan spoke, Linn nodded down at her. Meanwhile, a thought was busy forming itself in my befuddled head.

"…and, y'see, there was this boy Joe there, and he didn't know I was only fifteen and that I don't really drink, and he said he was going to the bar, and did I want a beer and I just said yes!" explained Rowan, her hands flapping in mid-air as she babbled.

"So, *were* you drunk last Saturday when Billy saw you?" I asked her, as the realization finally dawned.

"I was … sort of, I suppose," said Rowan, turning her face sideways to look at me. "But I just wanted to escape for a while – stop worrying for a few hours. And so I ended up drinking a few beers!"

"*Did* you stop worrying?" Linn asked her in a very gentle, very un-Linn voice.

"Yeah, but then I felt absolutely terrible and ended up *barfing* on the pavement in front of all my friends, and I had to go back to Chazza's and try to sober up before I came home."

"So that's why you didn't get home till so late," I said, slotting the pieces of the mystery together.

"Yeah, and I had a horrible hangover the next day and then I ended up yelling at Dad, just when he's so miserable about money and everything, and I feel terrible, even though I've told him I'm sorry for shouting, and that's why I don't want him to know what's going on at school so please don't anyone tell him, please please Linn please Ally!"

She was off again, getting all her words in a big, panicky jumble.

"Well, we've got to tell Mr Bashir, Ro. We have to! Lisa and Tasha can't get away with—"

Rowan had slapped her hands over her face at the sound of our headmaster's name, and from somewhere underneath her hands, I could make out her saying, "They'll kill me!"

Linn looked over at me. I looked back. I didn't know what to say that could help.

"OK, don't worry, Ro. We'll work out another

152

way around this, I promise. Cross my heart and hope to die..."

Slowly, Rowan slithered her hands down her face and peered hopefully at Linn.

"Promise," Linn repeated. "Now, me and Ally are going to have to go back to school after lunch, but why don't you go to bed and try and have a sleep this afternoon? I'll explain you're ill to the office. And I'll try and work something out that doesn't get you in more trouble. Honest."

"She's all right," said Linn, coming back into the kitchen after she'd checked on Rowan. "I gave her the hot-water bottle and put her favourite picture of Johnny Depp beside her bed..."

"Good," I said, pushing over a sandwich I'd just made for Linn, in my effort to feel less helpless and a little bit more useful.

"Thanks," mumbled Linn, flopping down on to one of the wooden chairs.

"So..." I began. "What are we going to do to help Ro?"

"Well, first, we've got to work out a rota, so that one of us always walks her to and from school, so those two losers don't get a chance to get her on her own."

"And then?" I asked, feeling a wave of relief

wash over me as my Super-Star Sister (I've never said a bad word against her, honest) took control.

"And then," said Linn, "I haven't a clue, Ally…"

Chapter 19

THE DRESS REHEARSAL

Kyra, Sandie, Frankie and Eddie were all sitting on my bed, staring at me.

"Well?' I asked them, self-consciously giving them a twirl (and tripping over a row of trainers at the same time).

What I was trying to do – apart from fall over – was show them my current number-one choice of outfit for my try-out at the card shop the next day. I had on my black school-cords, my black school-shoes and one of my white school-shirts (i.e. I hadn't had to change very much – just undo my tie and chuck it over the chair in my room).

"What do you think?" I asked again, picking at the splodge of orange beaniness I had just spotted on one cuff.

"Nice!" smiled Sandie encouragingly.

"Boring," yawned Kyra, flopping back on to her elbows.

Eddie and Frankie didn't say anything. In fact, now that I was standing still and not doing anything interesting like twirling and stumbling, I seemed to have lost their attention altogether. Both of them were slowly closing their eyes and getting all zen-like while Kyra and Sandie got on with stroking one each. They were both purring so much that Dad must have had to put up the sound on the telly downstairs, just to drown them out.

"Why's it boring?" I asked Kyra defensively, even though I knew it was boring.

"It looks like it's your school uniform, just without the tie!" she snorted.

Urgh. She'd spotted it.

"Try my grey trousers!" said Sandie, taking them out of the plastic bag she'd brought round with her.

But even though I really liked Sandie's trousers, before the girls had come round tonight I'd already decided it was a bad idea to wear something I'd borrowed from one of them to the shop. I mean, what if I got the job? I couldn't wear Sandie's trousers every week, and I sure couldn't afford to get myself a pair the same...

Nope, I definitely had to come up with something from my own wardrobe. However cruddy that was.

"No, it's OK, Sandie – I'll just wear something of my own, even if it is *boring*," I replied, directing the last bit at Kyra.

"Oh, for goodness sake..." muttered Kyra, pushing herself off the bed. "Let me have a look through your stuff. You've got to have something better than that stupid school shirt."

I think Kyra was a bit huffy with me because I hadn't wanted to wear any of the tops she'd brought round. But honestly, was she listening to what I'd said? Did she understand that I was going to be selling old ladies birthday cards for their grandkids all day, not going *clubbing*? And I could never have worn one of those skin-tight things anyway, 1) because they were so humungously skin-tight that I didn't think I'd be able to *breathe* properly, and 2) I'd be so self-conscious, imagining that every customer who came in was staring at my chest and thinking, "Poor girl – is it a medical condition that's left her so flat-chested?".

Just as Kyra yanked open the nearest drawer and began to haul out all my clothes on to the floor, there was a knock at my bedroom door.

"Come in!" I called out, and saw Rowan's face peer round the door.

She looked more like Rowan today – she had her hair pulled into two fat, brown bunches, with giant sunflower hair-elastics holding them in place. I knew she hadn't worn them to school like that (she was still playing safe and dressing down), but at least if she was acting like her normal, weirdo self at home it was a good sign. Even though, as far as I knew, Linn hadn't come up with a plan to deal with the bullying yet, I think Rowan felt better just having told us both her deep, dark secret.

"Hi!" Rowan smiled round at us all. "Dad sent me up. He's doing some cheese on toast and wanted to know if any of you fancied some."

"Do you want some, Kyra, Sandie?" I asked my friends.

"Yep! Red sauce too, please!" said Kyra, still busy dragging out clothes.

"Yes, please!" nodded Sandie.

"Tomato sauce on yours too?" Rowan asked, as she hung on to the door and surveyed the room.

"If that's OK," Sandie replied, doing her usual ooh-I-don't-want-to-make-a-fuss! face. Like adding a splurt of tomato sauce would put my dad to too much trouble, I *don't* think.

"I'll have some too," I nodded, assuming that Rowan would disappear back downstairs now.

But instead, she hovered by the door, watching Kyra hold up a black long-sleeved T-shirt.

"Now *this* would look really good with your black trousers," said Kyra triumphantly. "All black is very plain, but *very* cool."

"What are you guys doing?" asked Rowan, her

eyes suddenly bright at the sight of something involving dressing up.

"I'm trying to decide what to wear at the shop tomorrow," I explained.

Rowan bit her lip and stared at the top Kyra was holding up, then stared at me.

"Hold on! I've got to show you what *I'm* wearing tomorrow, to this party I'm going to!"

And with that, she was gone. By the time she reappeared, a few minutes later, Kyra had me dressed in my all-black uniform, and was experimenting with pulling my hair up into a high ponytail. (She was pulling it so hard that it hurt; but I was too scared she'd think I was a wimp to moan about it.)

"Ta-daaaa!" announced Rowan, standing at the bedroom door with her arms outstretched.

She looked great, in Rowan kind of way. She was wearing the lilac butterfly T-shirt she'd bought the week before, and – since she was holding her arms so high – I caught a glimpse of her new, tinkly belly chain. I hadn't seen the skirt before – it was pink, fake suede with a sort of lacy effect round the bottom where holes had been punched out. I hadn't seen the bag she was holding before either: a really pretty, beaded number. One of those that are so small you could probably only fit a Lypsol and a pound coin for the bus in it. (I couldn't ever have one of those – I need a rucksack the size of an Arctic explorer's for all the rubbish *I* lug around with me.) At least I recognized what she was wearing on her feet – it was like those red velvet mules were super-glued to her feet.

"I won't have *these* in, of course, 'cause they don't really go," said Rowan, pointing at her sunflowers.

She was wearing clashing lilac, pink and red so far. What made her think that yellow wouldn't "go"? Especially since nothing else did...

"So what *are* you going to wear in your hair?" asked Sandie.

Thankfully, Kyra was keeping stum. I thought she might be her usual cheeky self and tell Rowan she should get checked out for colour blindness, but she didn't. Partly, I think it's because she still felt sorry for Rowan after seeing what had happened to her the day before, and actually – even though she's never said so – I think she kind of admires Rowan. Even though she always calls her my "weird sister", Kyra knows that Rowan's a bit of an outsider at school, and having felt like that herself often enough, I'm sure Kyra feels like they've got something in common.

"I've got these new butterfly clips. They're

covered in this sort of velvety stuff and they look so beautiful!" Rowan gushed, clapping her hands to her chest.

New.

New, new, new.

The word stuck in my head like it was a big, flashing neon sign.

"Ro? Rowan? Where are you?" Dad's voice drifted up from two flights below.

"Oh! I forgot!" gasped Rowan. "I'm supposed to be helping him with the cheese on toast!"

"Have you and the rest of your family never thought about buying her a *mirror*?" Kyra couldn't resist joking, once Rowan had closed the door and safely pattered off down the stairs.

"Ha, ha," I groaned, rolling my eyes up to the ceiling.

"Nah, she looked all right," Kyra smiled at me, to show she hadn't meant it. "She'd look great at a party – on Mars!"

Being mouthy – it's like a reflex with Kyra. But I'm getting used to it. Slowly.

"I really liked her skirt," Sandie chipped in. "Is it new?"

See? There was that "new" word again. And in our house, and in our financial circumstances, that was *not* a good word to hear.

"I don't know where she's getting the money for all this stuff," I blurted out. "I mean, I've never seen that bag either!"

"Maybe she's nicking it!" Kyra laughed. "Maybe Rowan's face is going to turn up on *Crimewatch* for shoplifting half the stores in Wood Green High Street!"

"*Kyra!*" I blasted out at her. "That's *not* funny! How can you make nasty jokes like that about my sister, after what she's been through?"

But you know something? Kyra had been right tonight when it came to my clothes. And now, it was crazy, but I had this horrible, tummy-wrenching feeling that she might just, maybe, *possibly* be right about this too...

Chapter 20

AND WHAT HAPPENS IF I PRESS THIS BUTTON HERE...?

It was going quite well. I'd only made three mistakes on the till (those machines make a terrible squealy noise when you press the wrong button), forgotten to give some woman her change (I had to chase her down the road to give her it back), and burnt out the element in the kettle when Mrs Merrill asked me to make us coffee (well, anyone can forget to put in water, can't they?).

OK, so it wasn't going *fantastically* well, but Mrs Merrill was really sweet to me about it. She just kept smiling and trilling away with her songs, in-between helping me sort out whatever mess I'd got into. And after turning to jelly and speaking in a wobbly voice to the first thousand customers, I'd finally started to relax a bit and even begun to enjoy my day at Something Special.

"Will you get paid for this?" Chloe asked, just a little bit *too* loudly, when her and Kellie came into the shop to see how I was doing.

"I don't know, I didn't ask," I hissed back,

willing them to go away. (Suddenly I realized how bugged Linn must have felt last Saturday when me and Tor tried to say hello...)

"Even if it's just a trial day, I still think you should get paid!" Chloe said sniffily, as if she knew everything there was to know about shops, just 'cause her dad ran one. In case she'd forgotten, my dad ran his own shop *too*.

"Well ... whatever," I shrugged, trying to tidy up a totally tidy rack of cards and looking over Chloe and Kellie's shoulders to check that Mrs Merrill wasn't shooting me a dirty look for having my friends in.

"Does she know yet?" Kellie suddenly asked me. "That you're only thir—"

"What about *this* one? It's very funny!" I practically yelped, covering up what Kellie was about to say by thrusting a card under her nose.

"Huh?" said Kellie, frowning down at the *Sorry to hear you're under the weather!* message.

"*No*," I whispered to Kellie, "she *doesn't* know how old I am yet, and she *won't* know, unless one of my friends blurts it out!"

"Ahhh!" sighed Kellie, getting my point, thankfully. "Sorry!"

Chloe rolled her eyes at me, just to let me know she understood what a goofball Kellie could be.

"Come on, Kel – let's go get a burger," said Chloe, steering her towards the door. "See you later, Ally!"

"See you!" I called after them as left, weak with relief that they'd finally gone.

Only I didn't feel relieved for long. There was Chloe and Kellie outside on the pavement, waving in at me through the big plate-glass window and pointing to someone else they'd just bumped into: Billy.

I widened my eyes at him as he grinned mischievously at me.

Go away! I mouthed silently at him.

Mrs Merrill didn't see all the commotion behind her; she was standing at the counter, her back to the window, tra-la-la-ing away while she studied some order-form thing.

Outside, Billy was busy puckering up his mouth, and had put one hand on his hip while the other one seemed to be stroking an imaginary hat or something. Except...

Omigod. He was stroking an imaginary *wig*. His rotten impersonations didn't stop at his Maths teacher; he was doing Mrs Merrill now.

Go away! I mouthed more urgently. *Now*!

Oh boy. I could really see how I'd wound up Linn last week. I was so, so sorry. This was karma, paying me back for letting Tor dribble hamster food all over the carpet of the clothes shop and thinking it was quite funny...

Outside, I could now see that Billy, Chloe and Kellie were doubled up laughing. There was only one thing I could do (apart from praying Mrs Merrill wouldn't turn round), and that was to ignore them. I deliberately mussed up a whole row of cards – shovelling them together like a deck of cards – just to give myself the task of sorting them out.

A few minutes later, I dared to look round ... and saw no-one outside at the window. My shoulders sagged in relief. Chloe must have appealed to Billy's better nature (i.e. tempted his stomach with the news that they were going for a burger). At last, I was safe.

For about five minutes.

"Hi, Ally!" said Rowan brightly, as she and Tor stumbled into the shop, laden with bags of cat litter and hamster bedding. (Since I was busy today, Rowan had stepped into my much more sensible shoes and taken over Saturday Pet-Shop Duties with our little brother.)

"Um, hello..." I smiled at the two of them.

Mrs Merrill gave me a look – I didn't know whether it was an annoyed look or a curious look, but I thought I'd better do something.

"Mrs Merrill," I began, deciding that she'd be less irritated with my visitors if she knew this lot were family and not school buddies. "This is my sister Rowan and this is my brother Tor."

"Ooh, hello!" simpered Mrs Merrill, smiling first at Rowan but saving the bulk of her beaming smile for Tor. "We've spoken on the phone, haven't we, young man?"

Tor nodded wordlessly. I noticed that his eyes were glued not to Mrs Merrill's face, but to her head.

"And what have you been up to? What's in that heavy looking bag of yours?"

"Litter," muttered Tor, still gazing at her head.

Oh, please, Tor, I said to myself, *please stop staring at her wig!*

"Litter?" tittered Mrs Merrill. "You're such a good boy that you've been picking up other people's rubbish?"

"No, *litter*," said Tor, not getting her joke. "For cats to poo in."

Mrs Merrill seemed delighted by his response and tittered away some more.

Rowan gave me a little smile and a wink, then wandered off to look at cards.

"Mrs Merrill was only teasing you, Tor," I

explained, standing aside as a customer came through the door.

"Oh," Tor shrugged, staring up at me with his huge, brown eyes.

"So you've got a cat, have you, poppet?" Mrs Merrill beamed down at him, her blonde tower of fake curls teetering over him.

All of a sudden, Tor's eyes lit up and I knew that he was going to do what he never usually does much of – talk. There's only one subject that gets him yakking, and that's animals. And now that Mrs Merrill had unconsciously triggered the pet conversation, I knew the floodgates would open.

"I haven't got one cat, I've got *five*," he started babbling. "And their names are Colin and Frankie and Eddie and Derek and Fluffy. Colin only has three legs because—"

I hoped Mrs Merrill had a spare five hours, 'cause that was how long it was going to take to get through every single fluffy, scaly or feathered thing that lived in our house, as well as its individual history. Luckily for me – who knew it all inside out and back to front – the customer needed to be served.

" 'Scuse me!" I smiled at Mrs Merrill, as I slipped behind the counter and made for the till (with my fingers crossed that I wouldn't mess up this time).

"Ooh! Awwww! Really? Aw bless!" I heard Mrs Merrill comment after each pet's CV had been explained.

"Bye!" I said to the customer, as they left with their card *and* correct change (result!).

But then I noticed something.

Mrs Merrill was still smiling, but her smile was fading fast. Also, she didn't seem so entranced by the cuteness of my little brother. I followed her gaze, which was focused on something at the back of the shop.

Cricking my neck slightly, I bent over where I stood, to see what exactly Mrs Merrill could see.

Maybe she's nicking it! Maybe Rowan's face is going to turn up on Crimewatch *for shoplifting!* I heard Kyra's words from the night before ringing in my ears.

I'd been so wrapped up in work today that I'd conveniently put that whole, horrible conversation to the back of my mind. But it couldn't help springing forward now; not when I was watching Rowan stuff a birthday card into the pocket of her old, moth-eaten, leopard-print coat...

Chapter 21

FIRST-AID HOT CHOCOLATE

You know how some shops have those OPEN and CLOSED signs? Well, Mrs Merrill had another one. I was still standing, with my neck cricked, and Tor was still babbling on (about Mad Max, our thug of a hamster), when I saw Mrs Merrill step back, grab something from below the counter, and slap it on the door.

I caught a glimpse of it before she stuck it on – it was a white envelope with BACK IN 5 MINUTES! scrawled on it, and it already had a curly, old bit of Sellotape attached to the top.

As soon as she'd done that, Mrs Merrill flipped the Yale lock on the door. It looked like Something Special was most definitely shut.

"...and my stick insects all came from ... um..."

Tor was fading out now – now that he'd realized Mrs Merrill wasn't listening any more. And that she'd started to look very serious.

"Ally," she said to me, patting her wig just as

Billy had imitated minutes before, "Ally, I think we need to go through to the back office for a chat. *All* of us. *Especially* your sister..."

The back office still had the metallic smell of burnt kettle hovering around, and that just made the atmosphere all the more brittle and horrible as Mrs Merrill started telling Rowan off for stealing the card.

Me and Tor stood speechless by the office door, as Rowan sobbed and Mrs Merrill ranted. It was miserable beyond words to have to hover there and listen to it all. Even the sight of Mrs Merrill's wig slipping to one side as she ranted didn't help.

Rowan was *so* in the wrong that I knew I couldn't stick up for her in any way, so all I did was stand with my face staring down at the floor, give Tor's hand a big, comforting squeeze, and wish this could all be over *soon*.

"...well, all I can say is that you're very, very lucky I'm not calling the police!" I heard Mrs Merrill say suddenly.

Oh, thank *goodness*...

I flicked my gaze around at Rowan, but I think she was sobbing too much to have heard. Right then, I felt I could spontaneously combust, I was so hot with the stress of it all. (I could just see

171

the headlines in the local paper: *Crouch End Girl Spontaneously Combusts In Shoplifting Drama!* Wonder if there was a chance that story would turn up in a newspaper wherever Mum was, and get her hurrying back home to us?)

"Th – thank you!" I stuttered, speaking for both of us.

"That's all right, Ally," Mrs Merrill nodded majestically.

(If I'd been in the mood, I'd have said she suddenly reminded me of the Queen Mother, only with one of that big-boobed country singer Dolly Parton's wigs on. But the only mood I was in was to *kiss* Mrs Merrill, I was so grateful.)

"Rowan's really sorry, aren't you, Rowan?" I prompted my sister.

But Rowan was *way* too crumpled and soggy to respond.

"Well, maybe she is sorry and maybe she isn't," sighed Mrs Merrill, "but one thing's for sure – I think you'd all better go now."

"Thank you, Mrs Merrill," I whispered, grabbing my jacket and bag off the coat hook on the wall.

At the same time, I grabbed Rowan, who was going to be dribbling runny mascara on the floor soon, the way *she* was going.

"Thank you! And sorry!" I babbled to Mrs

Merrill, as I pushed Rowan in front of me, towards the front of the shop.

"Bye, Ally. Bye, Tor, dear," Mrs Merrill replied straight-faced, as she held the door open for us and blatantly ignored my sister.

"Thanks…" I heard myself whisper, as the door closed behind us.

"Oh, Ally! What have I done!" snuffled Rowan, dragging her feet along the pavement.

You've just lost me my job, I thought, though I didn't say it out loud. Rowan was awash with guilt at the moment and me piling on more wouldn't make things any better.

And anyway, it wasn't like I was the goody-goody sister in all this – I *had* tried to get the job under false pretences, after all. And when I thought about it, it was probably for the best. I wasn't going to be fourteen for *ages*, so if I *had* ended up working in Something Special, I'd have spent every Saturday feeling sick, just *waiting* to be found out.

"What have I done?" I heard Rowan repeat under her breath.

Rowan was a mess, there was no doubting that. But what about poor Tor, who'd had to witness all the horribleness? I glanced down and saw that he was looking a little shell-shocked round the edges.

Now, Grandma had once told me some old

wives' tale about shock … something dopey about sugary tea or something. Well, *stuff* the tea – I knew of something better.

"Come on!" I said in my best schoolteacher voice, putting a hand behind the backs of both Rowan and Tor. "It's Saturday, and you've just been to the pet shop. And Tor – do you want to tell Rowan what we always do for a treat after we've been to the pet shop?"

"Shufda's!" squeaked Tor, a smile (thankfully) breaking out on his face.

"What for?!" I prompted him.

"Hot chocolate!" he positively grinned.

"Ally, I think I – hic! – I should maybe just go home…" Rowan whimpered some more.

The benefit of Rowan being as limp as a rag doll meant that I could totally ignore what she was saying and gently steer her through the door of the café and over to a formica table that was tucked nicely out of sight at the back.

Right then, I knew what was best for her, and that was to sit and get a hold of herself before we got back to the house. OK, so Dad was round at the bike shop, and Linn would be busy trying to sell over-priced clothes to women with too much money weighing them down, but Grandma was going to be there doing one of her "spring cleans", which happened about once a month, whether it was spring, summer, autumn or doodah. And I *had* to get Rowan looking less hysterical before we could face Grandma...

"Is she OK?" the bloke who ran Shufda's whispered to me, as he placed our steamy mugs in front of us.

I could understand why he was worried, considering Rowan was hugging a plastic carrier bag of hamster bedding like it was some kind of hay-scented comfort blanket.

"She's fine," I whispered back, trying to nod reassuringly.

"Mmm, this is nice..." Rowan murmured in a teeny-tiny voice, slightly calmer now that she'd sat for a couple of minutes and taken her first sip of hot chocolate.

She even started slackening her grip on the hamster bedding.

It was all right; she was starting to come out of it. I felt like I could – just about – ask her the dreaded question.

"Why did you do it, Ro?" I asked quietly, so no-one at the other tables, eating their eggs and bacon, could hear.

"I... I ... wanted to take a card to Carla's birthday party tonight – even if I couldn't afford to buy her a present," she whispered, keeping her mascara-smudged eyes fixed on her hot chocolate.

"But Dad would have given you money for a card, Rowan!" I said to her. "We're not so skint that he couldn't let you have *that* much!"

Then – uh-oh – something else occurred to me. I hoped there was enough money left over from the pet-shop shopping to pay for these hot chocolates ... or we were going to be in big, big trouble for the second time in ten minutes. *And* find ourselves banned from going near the shops in the Broadway ever again.

Billy calls Tor "Spook Kid", and right that second, he lived up to his nickname. Reading my mind (or seeing me staring at the three mugs in a panic), Tor rummaged in his pocket and took out a handful of coins. Phew...

Now that we weren't going to be arrested for drinking stolen hot chocolate, I could concentrate on Rowan again.

"Ro..." I began. "Um ... have you ... have you ever shoplifted before?"

Rowan darted her anxious, dark eyes at me, and I could see the splodges of red flood into her cheeks. She knew I was talking about the purple sunglasses. And the beaded bag. And the belly chain. And that little pink skirt. And possibly other stuff that I hadn't even seen yet...

For a second Rowan said nothing, then it all came rushing out in a big, rambly burble.

"Oh, Ally! I didn't mean to! But I've been so totally miserable with Lisa and Tasha always having a go at me that I – I guess I just wanted to cheer myself up, y'know, with pretty things, and I know that sounds stupid now but I wasn't really thinking straight 'cause I was so stressed out and well, we're so poor right now and I didn't dare ask Dad for any extra money so I – oh God! – so I stole some stuff and ... and I can't believe I did it and please don't tell Dad please!"

While my brain was busy getting in a tangle with all this latest information, Rowan seemed to notice Tor for the first time in ages.

"Oh, Tor!" she squeaked, getting all dewy-eyed again. "Poor Tor! You had to see all that! I'm *so* sorry!"

Tor suddenly found his head in a vice-like arm lock, as Rowan cuddled our little brother to death. I knew how bad she must have been feeling; she and Linn and I have this kind of pact about keeping bad stuff away from Tor, since he's just a little kid and everything. But even if she was feeling bad, I knew I was going to have to prise her arms away from him in a second, before his face went *blue*.

"S'okay!" Tor managed to say, as he wriggled free from her bear hug, all by himself.

"Are you angry with me for being such a stupid idiot of a sister?" Rowan blinked at him pleadingly.

Tor picked up a serviette from the table – one that was only slightly soggy with hot-chocolate spills – and dabbed at Rowan's dribbly nose.

"Those girls you said – are they bullying you?" he asked her, obviously having picked up on the Lisa and Tasha remark.

Rowan gave him a wordless nod.

"So you stole things because you were feeling bad?"

Rowan nodded again.

"Well, bullying is very, very bad, but so is stealing."

"I know," muttered Rowan.

"You have to promise *never* to do it again," he said simply.

"I will. I mean, I won't," said Rowan, giving him a wobbly smile.

"*Ever*."

"Never ever, cross my heart," whispered Rowan, doodling a finger over her leopard-print coat.

"Good girl."

Good grief.

I'd always thought that Tor would end up as a World-Wildlife-Fund scientist studying equatorial anteaters or stuff like that, but the way he was going today, he could start a job as an Agony Uncle in one of the magazines I read.

"So ... ready to go home now?" I asked Rowan, who was looking almost like her normal self, apart from the red-rimmed eyes and matching nose. But we could always say she was coming down with a cold, or bubonic plague or something.

"Yep, I'm ready," said Rowan, taking a deep breath.

"Sure you don't want to tell Grandma?" I asked tentatively. "At least about the bullying stuff, I mean?"

Rowan shook her head hard. "Oh no! She'll just tell Dad and I don't want to worry him! Anyway, Linn'll think of a plan..."

I nodded in agreement – and crossed my fingers *really* tight under the table.

Chapter 22

LINN'S CUNNING PLAN. AND MINE.

Despite everything (and despite Grandma and Dad being slightly suspicious of how polite and lovely all of us were being to each other) it was quite a nice weekend.

When we'd arrived home, I'd had to tell Grandma a bit of a white lie about the job. Feeling my left eyelid start doing one of those telltale twitches, I launched into some story about how I'd got it wrong; how the try-out with Mrs Merrill was only a couple of hours, not a whole day, and how I didn't think I'd got it anyway because I made lots of mistakes on the till and destroyed the shop kettle (at least *that* much was true).

Then Grandma – who was on her hands and knees doing something with bleach inside the cupboard under the sink – sat up straight, pinged at the fingers of her yellow rubber gloves and said to me straight, "Well, Ally, you weren't really old enough to be doing it anyway, were you?"

Urgh, so much for thinking no-one in my family

had spotted that one.

"I know you were only trying to get a job to help your dad out, Ally, dear," she said, giving me a knowing look. "But I think it's worked out for the best, don't you?"

I nodded and started backing out of the kitchen. I felt a little unnerved, to tell you the truth, and I didn't want Mrs X-ray-eyes to see into my brain and suss out Rowan's secrets stored in there.

After that, me, Rowan and Tor took Winslet and Rolf for a long, long walk up around Highgate Woods (the dogs were deliriously happy about that, although the walk home got a bit much for Winslet's fun-size legs and Rowan and I had to take turns carrying her).

That evening, Rowan went out to her friend Carla's party, wearing – I noticed – the lilac butterfly T-shirt, but with some of her old stuff; not the pink skirt or bag or anything. (She also wasn't wearing her velvet mules, but that was because they were covered in mud. I *did* tell her they weren't going to be any good for stomping round a wood in, but she didn't listen...)

She came home really early from the party though. The next day, when me, Linn and Tor were playing Mousetrap with her (Tor's favourite game, though he does get a bit upset when the mouse gets trapped at the end), Rowan told us that she hadn't really been able to enjoy herself at the party, what with, y'know, *everything*.

Linn – who did, by now, know everything too, since I'd insisted Rowan told her, if no-one else – smiled a lot and was very nice to Rowan. But she still said nothing about a plan, and I didn't want to hassle her by asking about it.

So that was the weekend, which, by the way, turned out especially good when Dad announced he'd sold a whole family four bikes, and could pay off the bulk of the bills.

But now it was Monday morning, and it was not so wonderful. Me and Rowan were walking to school together, and both of us were stony silent. Rowan, 'cause I knew she was facing another day of dread, wondering what torturous little treats those creeps Lisa and Tasha had in store for her next; me, 'cause I knew *that* was what she was thinking. And, for once, I couldn't come up with a single thing that might cheer her up.

I lost sight of Rowan once we got to school and had to go into assembly. (You know how it is: you're meant to sit with your class. Who knows why.) For a second, I was distracted from worrying about Rowan as I filed my way into a row and saw Kyra sitting right between Chloe and Jen. And –

most peculiarly – it didn't look like Chloe wanted to kill her.

"How's your sister?" asked Sandie, as my other mates bent forward to listen, concern etched on all their faces.

"OK," I nodded quickly, seeing that Mr Bashir, the Headteacher, was striding up to the rostrum.

Everyone straightened up, before our Year Head – the mean-faced Mrs Fisher – gave us the evil eye.

"What's going on with *them*?" I whispered to Sandie, keeping my eyes front.

She knew what I meant. I mean, seeing Kyra sitting quite happily in amongst the rest of my mates was as unexpected as finding my mum at home, making the tea (I wish).

"Chloe says she thinks Kyra's OK, you know; after the way she helped out when your sister was chucked in the boys' loos," Sandie whispered back, in that way that's so quiet that only ultra-sonic radar and best friends can pick up.

Well, there was one good thing to come out of the misery Rowan had been through. Maybe I would be able to start inviting Kyra along to our Girls' Film Nights...

We couldn't whisper any more – Mr Bashir had started talking. To be honest, I think he's a pretty nice guy – a million times better than rotten teachers like Mrs Fisher – but I couldn't help going off into a dream when he was talking at assembly. Sometimes I wake up when he makes a joke or something (they're usually pretty bad, but pretty good for a teacher), and sometimes he does have the occasional interesting thing to say (like "There's going to be a school dance", or "The boiler isn't working so if the temperature drops too low we'll have to sent you all home early" or something just as fascinating).

But today, I really woke up. I mean, *really*. And it was all because Mr Bashir had started talking about … *bullying*. I listened to him as he went on about how he'd heard bullying was really bad at other schools in our area, and speaking about the heavy-duty punishments bullies get there. Then he said that he hadn't heard of any bullying lately at *our* school, but if he did, then he'd have to deal with people just as harshly as the other headteachers did.

I felt Sandie poke me in the leg with her finger, and I gave her a little nod in reply. What Mr Bashir was saying was brilliant; now he was even saying stuff about how people shouldn't be hassled because they're different, and all the time mentioning no-one in particular. I really, really wanted to look round the hall and see if I could see Lisa Dean or Tasha Franklin, but I didn't dare.

Please! I thought. *Please let them get the message, if they're not too brain-dead for it to sink in…*

Me and Rowan were just about to turn out of the gates and go home for lunch, when we heard Linn calling after us.

"Wait up!" she panted, leaving her friends behind and hurrying over to join us.

"Won't you be late for school dinners, Linnhe?" asked Rowan. "Won't you miss getting the best table?"

Linn waved back as her friends Mary and Nadia trotted off without her. "Nah, I thought I'd come home with you guys for a change," she shrugged.

Wow. All this stuff with Rowan really had changed things. Not only was Linn dodging out of school dinners with her mates to hang out with us, but she hadn't even got annoyed with Rowan for using her whole name.

"So, Rowan," said Linn, checking the road before we crossed. "How's it been going with Lisa and Tasha so far today?"

"OK, I suppose," replied Rowan, following Linn and me as we darted between the traffic. "I saw them a couple of times, but they just blanked me."

"That's pretty good, isn't it?" Linn smiled at her.

"Definitely better than getting shoved in a toilet," I joined in, trying to make Rowan laugh.

And she did, for about the first time in a *year*. (Well, OK, it was just over a week, but it *felt* more like a year.)

Linn shot me a pleased look.

"Hey, Linn," I said, about to hit my big sister with a question that had been floating round my head all morning. "Did you have something to do with what Mr Bashir said in assembly this morning?"

"Course I did!" she answered matter-of-factly. "I went to see him on Friday afternoon; told him exactly what was going on with Ro but said that she was too scared to get those two drongos into trouble. And so we came up with a plan for him to say that stuff today. Y'know, shaming them without naming them – at least that's what he called it."

"But why didn't you tell me you were going to do that?" asked Rowan, looking more than a little bit gobsmacked.

"Because knowing *you*, I thought you'd freak out," Linn explained. "I thought you'd be too worried and mortified to go to assembly if I told you."

That was true, I thought to myself. *Mind you, she could have let* me *in on the secret...*

But I sure wasn't going to be petty about it, not when it seemed to have worked. I mean, it was early days, but if Lisa and Tasha had ignored Rowan this morning, specially after what they'd done to her last Friday, then it *must* be a good omen.

"Thanks, Linnhe!" Rowan blinked at her.

God, she wasn't going to cry again, was she?

"Hold on," said Linn, stopping where she was on the pavement.

Me and Rowan stopped too, and wondered what was going on.

"There, that's better!" grinned Linn, reaching round and pulling the scrunchie out of Rowan's plain ponytail and letting her hair tumble loose. "That looks more like you now! What about sticking in some of your stupid butterfly clips when we get home, so everyone recognizes you?"

Instead of making Rowan smile again, that last little comment of Linn's made her go all pancake flat for some reason.

"What's up?" I frowned at her.

"I just remembered ... those new clips, and all the other stuff that I ... I ... that I..."

"Stole?" I suggested.

OK, it was a bit blunt but someone had to say it if Rowan found it too difficult.

"Yeah, that," she nodded, steering herself around the word. "Well, they're all stuffed in a bag under my bed. What am I going to do with them? I can't wear any of it!"

OK, so far today, Linn had done an amazing job at helping Rowan out. But now it was my turn for a bright idea.

"Come on," I said marching towards the post office in the parade of shops.

"What are we doing?" asked Linn, following behind me.

"You can remember where all the bits came from? Everything you stole, I mean?" I turned and asked Rowan.

Wincing, she nodded.

"Then we are going to buy a whole pile of padded brown envelopes and stamps," I announced, "and then we're going to spend lunchtime packaging everything up and sending them back. With notes saying sorry."

Rowan looked a bit alarmed.

"You don't have to sign them, silly," I grinned at her. "We'll do it anonymously!"

"*That*," Linn beamed at me, "is the most *brilliant* idea, Ally!"

Well, there's a first time for everything, and Linn praising me like that sure was a first.

But don't get too excited. After Rowan's little drama, everything slowly got back to normal in the Love household. Dad managed to pay the bills and we've gone back to being just slightly skint, instead of super-skint. Rowan's begun to wear her usual selection of bizarre clothes and hairstyles, and – thankfully – Lisa and Tasha don't do any more than throw her dirty looks these days. And after being the best, nicest, friendliest big sister anyone could have, Linn has gone back to being her usual grumpy self, slagging off Rowan's (rotten) attempts at cooking, and never praising me for a thing ever since.

Speaking of Linn, I've got to go – she'll be back in from her Saturday job soon and I'd better chase any random pets out of her room. I left the door open when I sneaked through and borrowed a pen to write all this stuff down, and someone hairy is bound to have taken advantage and sneaked on to her pristine white duvet for a snooze.

Uh-oh – too late... I can hear Linn stomping up the stairs. And now she's yelling at Winslet, telling her to drop her Wonderbra and drop it NOW!

And there they go – Winslet's claws are pattering down the stairs while Linn thunders after her, growling. (Linn, not Winslet, in case you were wondering.)

Ah, home sweet home...

* * *

PS And the moral of the story is ... if you're being bullied, you've got to do *something* about it. Even if that just means imagining whoever's bullying you sitting with their knick-knacks round their ankles on the loo. There, feel better already?

PPS Hope Grandma never reads this: she'd be like, "Oh, Ally, do you *have* to be so disgusting?" And the answer is ... yes!

Look out for

FRIENDS, FREAK-OUTS AND VERY SECRET SECRETS

"Maybe he isn't coming," Sandie suggested.

"He'll come. He *always* comes," I replied, keeping my eye on the silvery white plane cruising by overhead.

It was going to ... Santa Fe, I decided, settling for today's fantasy destination. I could be up there on that plane now, flicking through my *Rough Guide to New Mexico* – my dream boy (Alfie, natch) in the next seat – instead of sitting on a park bench getting splinters in my bum and a crick in my neck.

"Maybe he's forgotten," I heard Sandie continue.

"Billy won't forget. We do this every Sunday morning."

Yep – every Sunday, whether it's rain or shine, whether I'm tired or not, I trudge up to the bench me and Billy call home (around 11 a.m. on a Sunday, anyway), high up on the grassy banks of the park, with Ally Pally at my back and the high-rise pointy bits of central London off on the horizon in front of me.

By my side are Rolf and Winslet (the reason I *have* to come, rain or shine, tired or not). And either Billy will be here already, or he'll be on his way, to catch up and gossip with me, while his monstrously annoying little dog spends quality time driving *my* dogs mad.

OK, so Sandie doesn't usually join us, but she does know that's the routine. So how come – this one time when she'd tagged along – was she supposing that Billy wouldn't show?

"Maybe he's busy or something."

I stopped looking skyward and turned to look at my best friend instead.

"If he was busy, he'd have phoned," I said, wondering what she was getting at.

"Yeah, but maybe he's so busy with something that he hasn't noticed the time," she shrugged. "And that would be all right, because then it would just be the two of us and—"

"*Aaaaarrghhhhh!!!*"

Billy arrived with a roar and a thump, as he leapt over the back of the bench to join us.

Rolf and Winslet found this extremely exciting. There was a general scuffle of barking and hairy paws as they jostled for position, both of them desperate to clamber all over him and lick his face. I was also pleased to see Billy, but didn't feel the need to lick his face. Instead, I just grinned.

"Can't you just walk up and say hello, like a normal person?" I asked him.

"Why?" Billy replied, blinking at me from below the peak of his baseball cap.

Fair enough. There wasn't a rule book around that said Billy had to act normal if he didn't want to.

"Is that new?" I asked, tugging at the cap till it came down over his face.

Billy had about a million baseball caps. Looked like he'd just bought his millionth-and-*one*.

"Yep," he mumbled from behind it. "It's Nike. Got it yesterday. Hi, Sandie, by the way!"

He waved at her, although he couldn't see her. Well, not till I pulled the cap off and tried it on for myself.

Maybe it was the fact that I was nicking something from his master, or maybe it was just the way Billy's hair was sticking up that frightened him, but Precious the not-at-all-precious poodle went into yapping overload.

Yappitty-yappitty-yappitty-yap-yap-yap!

"I thought baseball caps were out of fashion now," said Sandie, over the top of the noise.

"Dunno," shrugged Billy. "Don't care. Shut up,

Precious! Go away! Go and play with Rolf and Winslet!"

"Since when have *you* cared about what's in fashion?" I laughed at Sandie.

I didn't mean it horribly, I just meant that she's the same as me when it comes to clothes and stuff – we like keeping up with what's in the magazines, but we don't exactly want to *shoot* ourselves if we can't afford the latest kitten-heeled *wellies* or whatever is "in". In fact, we are both guilty of sniggering quite a bit at some of the fashion junkies we see wandering around the shops on Saturday afternoons. You know, those people who look like they're trying so hard to be cutting edge with their clothes that they're just kind of *sad*.

Anyway, like I said, the remark about not caring about what's in fashion; I didn't mean it horribly. But Sandie seemed to take it that way.

"Are you saying I'm not trendy or something?" she blinked at me, her vast blue eyes extra-wide and full of hurt.

Uh-oh.

"No, of course not!" I protested.

Wow, she can be *so* touchy sometimes.

Yappitty-yappitty-yap-yap-yap-yap-yap-yap!

Turning away from Sandie, I yanked the baseball cap off my head and stuck it back on the bonce of its rightful owner – hoping that might shut Precious up.

It didn't.

Yip-yip-yippetty-yap-yap-yap-yap-yap!

"What's *wrong* with him?" I asked Billy, staring down at the barking ball of fluff in front of us.

"I think he just wants to play," Billy mumbled, straightening his cap, since I'd rammed it on sideways.

Hat sorted, he bent forward and scooped up Precious in both hands, turning the dog round to face my hairy hounds, who were now stretched out and panting on the grass.

As if he had the brain of a battery-operated toy, Precious now totally forgot us and started yapping directly at Rolf and Winslet. I wished for a second that he *was* battery-operated – that way there might be a volume control on him somewhere that I could turn down.

"So, how come you're here today, Sandie? Just desperate to see me?" Billy grinned mischievously.

From the other end of the bench, Sandie made a little tutting sound and blushed silently.

Here we go – the usual way my two best mates communicate, or *don't* communicate, to be more accurate. In front of Sandie, Billy gets cheekier and more show-offy than normal, and that makes

Sandie get shyer (and quieter) than normal. And that makes it really hard work for *me* – trying to keep a lid on Billy being silly and trying to drag Sandie into the conversation whether she likes it or not.

"Very funny, ha, ha," I said sarcastically. "Sandie stayed over last night, and just fancied hanging out for a while, didn't you, Sandie?"

"Mmmmm," Sandie nodded, keeping her gaze fixed on the three dogs playing (and, in grumpy Winslet's case, growling) in front of us.

"Yeah, my Grandma brought her boyfriend, Stanley, round to visit last night," I continued, keeping Billy up to date with the latest events in the world of Love. "It was pretty funny – I think he got a bit freaked out by Rowan's cooking—"

"No wonder!" grunted Billy.

"—and then, when Tor cut his pizza into the shape of a beard and moustache and tried to wear it, you should have seen his face! It was pretty funny, wasn't it, Sandie?"

"Yeah," nodded Sandie.

"And the poor guy – it turns out he's allergic to animals, and he'd taken this anti-histamine tablet to stop him sneezing and everything," I continued, turning my head to face Billy again, "but it didn't work – not against our zoo! He was snotting all over the place by the time they left, wasn't he, Sandie?"

I turned to face her.

"Uh-huh," was all I got for my efforts.

And so it went on.

Billy told us about football practice the day before, and demonstrated – in slow motion – how he scored the winning goal (see what I mean about the showing-off thing?) He told us about these three girls who hung around and watched, whistling at the lads and generally annoying them (a lie, I'm sure – I bet all the guys *loved* it). He even told us about the lad on his team who'd cleverly managed to stop a pass at goal by letting the ball collide with his *nose*, and how amazing it was that so much blood came out of it. (Apparently the girls disappeared pretty quick after that, looking a bit white-faced.)

The way Billy told it, with lots of acting out and exaggeration, it kind of made me laugh. Sandie? Well, Sandie didn't seem to manage much more than a limp smile here and there.

Maybe she wasn't feeling very well and just didn't want to say anything in front of Billy, I decided.

"Oh, and I forgot to tell you," said Billy, dragging my thoughts back to him.

"What?"

"Well, I saw Richie at football yesterday, and he said he wants to talk to you."

"Richie/Ricardo?" I asked, frowning. "Kyra's Richie/Ricardo?"

From what I'd seen of my mate Kyra's on-off boyfriend (currently *off*), he had all the charm of a doorknob. He might have tried to make himself sound more impressive by introducing himself as "Ricardo" to Kyra when they first met, but impressive, he was not. Big-headed, self-centred, slimy ... yep, all those words described him well. At least, that's how he came across to me. Billy (who knew him as Richie, like the rest of the world) thought he was kind of all right. Which made me think that Richie/Ricardo is one of those boys that can't handle girls as *people* – only things to snog.

"Yeah, Kyra's Richie!" Billy nodded at me.

"What does he want to talk to *me* for?" I asked, feeling myself go pink.

But Billy wasn't listening; he was watching the situation that had developed between our dogs...

"Winslet!" I shouted, seeing what was happening. "Put Precious down! *Now!*"

Grudgingly, Winslet opened her jaws, releasing the grip she had on the scruff of Precious's neck. She'd been determinedly stomping her four stubby legs in the direction of the nearest bin, dragging a whining Precious with her. I could be wrong, but it seemed to me like she was planning on flinging him inside it – maybe after one too many attempts to sniff her where the sun don't shine. Winslet may be a strange-looking dog (a cross between something big and hairy and something with sawn-off legs), but she does have her dignity.

"Hmm, maybe I should take him home," mused Billy, as Precious bounded into his arms, away from harm (i.e. Winslet).

"Hold on!" I said urgently. "You haven't told me what Richie/Ricardo wants to talk to me about yet!"

"Huh?" Billy frowned at me, as if he hadn't the faintest clue what I was on about.

Hopeless.

For a second, I felt like doing a Winslet and chucking *Billy* in the bin...

Also by Karen McCombie

Stella Etc.

To: You
From: Stella
Subject: Stuff

Hi there!

You'd think it would be cool to live by the sea with all that sun,
sand and ice cream. But, believe me, it's not such a breeze.
I miss my best mate Frankie, my terror twin brothers drive me
nuts and my mum and dad have gone daft over the country
dump, sorry, "character cottage", that we're living in. I'm
bored, and I'm fed up with being the new girl on the block.
Still, I quite fancy finding out more about the mysterious,
deserted house in Sugar Bay. And what's with the bizarre old
lady who feeds fairycakes to seagulls. . .?
Catch up with me (and my fat, psychic cat!) in the Stella Etc.
series.
LOL

stella
XXX

Want to know more. . .?

Check out Karen's super-cool website!

karenmccombie.com

For behind-the-scenes gossip on Karen's very own blog,
fab competitions and photo-galleries,
join her website of loveliness now!